"I was a virgin!"

"How was I supposed to know that? You're a twenty-six year old woman."

Pepe thought virgins of that age were extinct, a thought he kept to himself. Cara's skin had gone as red as her hair. He didn't particularly fancy being on the receiving end of a slap in front of his entire family, even if she would need a stepladder to reach him.

"You used me," she said. "You let me believe you were serious, and that we would see each other again."

"When? Tell me, when did I say we would see each other again?"

"You said you wanted me to come to your new house in Paris so I could advise you where to place the Cannelotti painting you brought in the auction."

He shrugged. "That was business talk. You know about art and I needed an expert's eye."

"You said it while dipping your finger in champagne and then placing it in my mouth so I could suck it off."

"What's done is done. I've apologized and as far as I'm concerned that's the end of the matter. It's been four months. I suggest you forget about it and move on."

With that, he stalked away, striding toward Luca and Grace, ready to tell them he was leaving.

"Actually, it's not the end of the matter."

Something in the tone of her voice made him pause.

"It's impossible for me to *forget about it and move on.*"

The Irresistible Sicilians

Dark-hearted men with devastating appeal!

These powerful Sicilian men are bound by years
of family legacies and dark secrets.

But now the power rests with them.

No *man* would dare challenge these
hot-blooded Sicilians....

But their women are another matter!

Have these world-renowned Sicilians met their match?

Read Luca Mastrangelo's story in

What a Sicilian Husband Wants

March 2014

Read Pepe Mastrangelo's story in

The Sicilian's Unexpected Duty

April 2014

And look out for Francesco Calvetti's story

Coming soon!

Michelle Smart

—

The Sicilian's Unexpected Duty

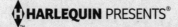
HARLEQUIN PRESENTS®

Recycling programs
for this product may
not exist in your area.

ISBN-13: 978-0-373-13238-6

THE SICILIAN'S UNEXPECTED DUTY

First North American Publication 2014

Copyright © 2014 by Michelle Smart

Printed in U.S.A.

All about the author...
Michelle Smart

MICHELLE SMART's love affair with books began as a baby when she would cuddle them in her cot. This love for all things wordy has never left her. A voracious reader of all genres, she says her love of romance was cemented at the age of twelve when she came across her first Harlequin® book. That book sparked a seed, and although she didn't have the words to explain it then, she had discovered something special—that a book had the capacity to make her heart beat as if falling in love.

When not reading or pretending to do the housework, Michelle loves nothing more than creating worlds of her own featuring handsome brooding heroes and the sparkly, feisty women who can melt their frozen hearts. She hopes her books can make her readers' hearts beat a little faster, too.

Michelle Smart lives in Northamptonshire with her own hero and their two young sons.

Other titles by Michelle Smart available in ebook:

WHAT A SICILIAN HUSBAND WANTS
(The Irresistible Sicilians)
THE RINGS THAT BIND

This book is dedicated to Adam, Joe and Zak,
my gorgeous Smarties.

CHAPTER ONE

PEPE MASTRANGELO HELPED himself to another glass of red wine from a passing maid and downed it in one. His aunt Carlotta, who had taken it upon herself to shadow him since they'd arrived back at his family home, was blathering on in his ear about something or other. Probably parroting her favourite inanities about when he, Pepe, was going to follow in his older brother's footsteps and settle down. Namely, when was he planning to get married and have babies?

Aunt Carlotta was not the only guilty party in this matter. The entire Mastrangelo clan, along with the Lombardis from his mother's side, all thought his private life was a matter of public consumption. Usually he took their nosiness in good part, knowing they meant well. He would deflect their questions with a cheeky grin, a wink and a quip about how there were so many beautiful women in the world he couldn't possibly choose just one. Or words to that effect. Anything but admit he would rather swim in a pool of electric eels than marry.

Marriage was for martyrs and fools, and he was neither.

He'd almost married once, when he'd been young and foolish. His childhood sweetheart. The woman who'd ripped his heart out, torn it into shreds and left an empty shell.

Now he considered that he'd had a lucky escape. Once bitten, twice shy. Only complete idiots went back for a second helping of pain if it could be avoided.

Not that he ever shared that little titbit of information with people. Heaven forbid. They'd probably try to talk him into something ridiculous like therapy.

Today though, his usually quick repartee had deserted him. But then, he wasn't usually fielding these questions with a pair of almond-shaped green eyes following his every move. To make it even harder to concentrate, those same eyes were drilling into him with pure loathing.

Cara Delaney.

He and Cara had been appointed his niece's godparents. He'd been forced to sit next to her in the church. He'd been forced to stand by her side at the font.

He'd forgotten how pretty she was—with her large eyes, tiny nose and small heart-shaped lips, she looked like a ginger geisha. Although *ginger* was the wrong word to describe the red flame of hair that fell down her back. Today, wearing a red crushed-velvet dress that showcased her curvy figure yet barely displayed an inch of flesh, she looked more than pretty. She looked incredibly sexy. Under normal circumstances he'd have no hesitation in spending the day in her company, flirting with her, plying her with drinks, maybe seeing if a repeat performance could be on the cards.

Being in the presence of his ex-lovers was not usually a problem, especially as his 'emotionally needy' detector was so acute. As a rule, he could spot a 'looking for marriage and babies' woman at ten paces and avoid her at all costs. As such, meeting up with an ex-lover was usually no big deal.

This time was different. Under normal circumstances he hadn't last seen them when he'd sneaked out of the hotel suite, leaving them sleeping in the very bed they'd just made love in. And usually he hadn't stolen their phone.

As soon as the date for the christening had been set a month ago, he'd known he would have to see Cara again. It was inconceivable that she wouldn't be there. She was his sister-in-law's best friend.

He'd expected the loathing that would be pointed his way. He really couldn't blame her for that. What he hadn't expected was to feel so… The word that would explain the strange sickness churning in his stomach wouldn't come. Whatever the word, he did not like it at all.

A quick glance at his watch confirmed he would have to endure her laser glare for another hour before he could leave for the airport. Tomorrow he'd be taking a tour of a profitable vineyard in the Loire Valley that he'd heard through the grapevine—pun intended—was being considered for sale. He wanted to get in there and, if viable, make an offer before any competitor started digging around.

'I *said*, she's beautiful, isn't she?' Aunt Carlotta's voice had taken a distinctly frosty tone. Somehow, in between her non-stop nattering, she had managed to acquire Lily without him noticing. She held the baby aloft for his perusal.

He peered down at the chubby face with the black eyes staring up at him, and all he could think was how like a little dark-haired piglet she looked. 'Yes, beautiful,' he lied, forcing a wide smile.

Seriously, how could anyone think babies were beautiful? Cute at a push maybe, but beautiful? Why anyone raved about them was beyond him. They were the most boring of creatures. He quite liked toddlers though. Especially when they were getting up to mischief.

He was saved from having to fake any more enthusiasm by a great-aunt barging him out of the way so she too could coo at the poor child.

Using this momentary lapse of Aunt Carlotta's attention, he sidled away.

Was this the way people acted at all christenings? From the way his relatives were behaving, anyone would think Lily had been conceived from a virgin birth. Having not attended a christening in nearly fifteen years, he wouldn't know. Given a chance, he would have got out of this one too. But there'd been no way, not when he'd been made godfather. Luca, his brother, would have strung him up if he'd tried to avoid it.

He wondered how long it would take for Luca and Grace to try again. No doubt they would keep trying until a boy was born. His own parents had struck gold from the outset, the need for an heir immediately satisfied with Luca's birth. Pepe's own conception was more along the 'spare' lines and to give Luca a playmate.

Was he being unfair to his parents? He didn't know or care. He'd been feeling out of sorts all day, and having the red-headed geisha glaring at him as if he were the Antichrist was not helping his mood.

Forget it, he thought, reaching for another glass of red from a passing maid. No one would notice if he left earlier than was deemed polite…

'You look stressed, Pepe.'

He muttered an expletive under his breath.

He should have known he wouldn't be able to escape without her collaring him. There had been something too determined in that expression of hers.

Plastering another fake smile on his face, he turned

around and faced her. 'Cara!' he exclaimed with bon-homie so fake even Lily would see through it. Grabbing her shoulder with his free hand, he pulled her into him and leaned down to kiss both her cheeks. She was so short he almost had to double over. 'How are you? Enjoying the party?'

Her dark coppery eyebrows knotted together into a glare. 'Oh, yes. I'm having a marvellous time.'

Pretending not to notice the definite edge to her voice, he nodded and raised the wattage of his grin. 'Fabulous. Now, if you'll excuse me, I have—'

'Running away again, are you?' Her Irish lilt had thickened since he'd last seen her. When they'd first met, here in Sicily three years ago, her voice had contained only the lightest of traces; by all accounts she'd left Ireland for England when she was a teenager. When he'd seduced her in Dublin four months ago, he'd noticed her accent had become more pronounced. Now there was no doubting her heritage.

'I have to be somewhere.'

'Really?' If an inflection could cut glass, that one word would have done the trick. She nodded her head in his sister-in-law's direction. 'She's the reason you stole my phone, isn't she?' It wasn't a question.

He drew in a breath before meeting Cara's stony glare. The last time he'd been with her, those eyes had been brimful of desire. 'Yes. She's the reason.'

Cara's geisha lips always drew a second glance—her bottom lip was beautifully plump, as if it had been stung by a bee. Now she drew it tightly under her teeth and bit into it. When she released it, the lip was a darker, even more kissable red. Her eyes had become a laser death stare.

'And was it my phone that led Luca to find her?'

There was no point in lying. She already knew the answers. Lying would demean them both. '*Sì.*'

'You came all the way to Dublin, to the auction house where I work, spent two million euros on a painting, and all to get hold of my phone?'

'*Sì.*'

She shook her head, her long copper locks whipping over her shoulders. 'I take it the whole "I've always wanted to visit Dublin, please show me around" thing was also deliberate?'

'Yes.' He held her icy gaze and allowed the tiniest of softening into his tone. 'I really did have a great weekend—you're an excellent tour guide.'

'And you're an unmitigated…' She buried the curse beneath a deep breath. 'But that's by the by. You seduced me for one reason and one reason only—so you could steal my phone the minute I fell asleep.'

'That was the main reason,' he agreed, experiencing the strangest tightening in his chest. 'But I can assure you, I enjoyed every minute. And I *know* you enjoyed it too.'

Cara had come undone in his arms. It had been an experience that still lingered in his memories and his senses, but an experience he ruthlessly dispatched from his head now.

All he wanted was to get away from her, get away from this claustrophobic party with all the talk of *babies* and *marriage*, and find himself a few hours of oblivion.

Her cheeks coloured but her jaw hardened. 'What's *enjoyment* got to do with anything? You lied to me. You spent a whole weekend lying to me, pretending to enjoy my company…'

He flashed his most winning smile. 'I did enjoy your company.' He certainly wasn't enjoying it now though.

This conversation was worse than the frequent visits to the headmaster he'd endured as a schoolboy. Just because he deserved someone's censure didn't mean he had to enjoy it.

'Do I look like I was born yesterday?' she shot back. 'The *only* reason you hooked up with me was because your brother was so desperate to find Grace.'

'My brother deserved to know where his wife had gone.'

'No, he did not. She's not his possession.'

'A lesson I can assure you he has learned. Look at them.' He nodded over to where Luca had joined his wife, his arms locked around her waist. Fools, the pair of them. 'They're happy to be back together. Everything has worked out for the best.'

'I was a virgin.'

He winced. He'd been trying his best to forget that little nugget. 'If it's an apology you're after then I apologise, but, as I explained at the time, I didn't know.'

'I told you…'

'You told me you'd never had a serious boyfriend before.'

'Exactly!'

'And as I told you before, not having a serious boyfriend does not equate to being a virgin.'

'It does—did—for me.'

'How was I supposed to know that? You're a twenty-six-year-old woman.' He'd thought virgins of that age were extinct, a thought he kept to himself. Cara's skin had gone as red as her hair. He didn't particularly fancy being on the receiving end of a punch in the face in front of his entire family, even if she would need a stepladder to reach him. There was something of a ferocious Jack Russell about her at that moment.

'You used me,' she said, almost snarling. 'You let me believe you were serious, and that we would see each other again.'

'When? Tell me, when did I say we would see each other again?'

'You said you wanted me to come to your new house in Paris so I could advise you where to place the Canaletto painting you bought in the auction.'

He shrugged. 'That was business talk. You know about art and I needed an expert's eye.' He still needed one; he'd bought his Parisian home to showcase his art collection, but the entire lot was still in storage.

'You said it while dipping your finger in champagne and then placing it in my mouth so I could suck it off.'

A flare of heat stirred in his groin. That particular moment had been during their last meal together, shortly before she'd agreed to join him in his hotel room and spend the night with him.

He cut his thoughts off the direction they were headed. The last thing he needed at that moment was to remember anything further about that night. It was becoming uncomfortable enough in his underwear as it was.

'Why didn't you steal my phone from the outset? Why string me along for a whole weekend?' Her eyes were no longer firing hostility at him. All he saw in them was bewilderment.

It had been easier dealing with Aunt Carlotta's jabbering mouth than with *this*. Okay, he got that Cara felt humiliated—he hardly recalled his actions that weekend with pride—but surely it was time for her to get over it?

'I couldn't steal your phone because you keep your handbag pressed so tightly to you I knew it would be impossible to steal.' Even now, she had the long strap placed diagonally over her neck and across her chest, the bag itself tucked securely under her arm.

'I'm surprised you didn't arrange for someone to mug me. I'm sure between you and your brother you know enough shady people to do the job. It would have saved you wasting a weekend of your precious time.'

'But you could have got hurt,' he argued silkily. A strange shiver rippled through his belly at the thought, a feeling dismissed before it was properly acknowledged.

He'd had enough. He'd behaved atrociously but it had been necessary. He wasn't prepared to spend the rest of the evening apologising for it. He'd never told her an actual lie—how she'd interpreted his words was nothing to do with him. 'You share a house with three other women, which made breaking into your home too risky, and you keep your phone on you when you're working. If you'd left your handbag unattended just once throughout that weekend, I would have taken it, but you didn't—you didn't let it out of your sight.'

'So now it's *my* fault?' she demanded, hands on hips.

Cara had to be one of the shortest people he'd ever met, certainly on a par with his great-aunt Magdalena. In the four months since he'd last seen her, she'd lost weight, making her seem more doll-like than he remembered. Yet, whether it was the long flaming hair or the ferocity blazing from her eyes, she stood tall and unapologetic before him, as if a tank would not be enough to knock her down.

He bit back another oath. 'What's done is done. I've apologised and as far as I'm concerned that's the end of the matter. It's been four months. I suggest you forget about it and move on.'

With that, he stalked away, striding towards Luca and Grace, ready to tell them he was leaving.

'Actually, it's not the end of the matter.'

Something in the tone of her voice made him pause.

'It's impossible for me to *"forget about it and move on"*.'

A shiver of something that could be interpreted as fear crawled up his spine...

Cara watched Pepe's back tense and all the muscles beneath his crisp pink shirt bunch together.

Only Pepe could get away with a pink linen shirt, unbuttoned at the neck, and snug-fitting navy chinos for his own niece's christening. The shirt wasn't even tucked in! Yet he still oozed masculinity. If she could, she'd rip all the testosterone from him—and there must be buckets of it—and flush it down the toilet. Standing next to him in the church, she had been acutely aware of how overdressed she looked in comparison, and had fumed at the unfairness of it all—*he* was the one underdressed for the occasion. With his long Roman nose, high cheekbones, trim black goatee covering his strong chin and his ebony hair quiffed at the front, Pepe looked as if he'd stepped off a catwalk.

She'd truly thought she'd been prepared. In her head she'd had everything planned out. She would be calm. She would politely ask for five minutes of his time, explain the situation and tell him what she wanted. Above all else, she would be calm.

Under no circumstances would she let him know of her devastation when she'd awoken alone in his hotel suite, or her terror when the stick in her hand had turned pink.

She would be calm.

All her good intentions had been thrown by the wayside when she'd taken one look at his handsome face and wanted to knock his perfect white teeth out.

The whole time she'd been next to him at the christening, even while they were making their respective promises as Lily's godparents, all she could think was how much she wanted to cause him bodily harm. She'd even found herself gazing at the silver scar that ran down his cheek, wishing she could track the culprit down and shake his hand. Or her hand. She'd asked Pepe about the scar during their weekend together but he'd evaded the question with his customary ease. She hadn't pushed the matter but it had tugged at her. All she'd wanted to do was trace a finger down it and make it magically disappear.

Who, she'd wondered, could have hated him enough to do such a thing? Pepe was charm personified. Everyone adored him. Or so she'd thought.

Now it wouldn't surprise her in the least to discover a queue of people wishing to perform bodily harm on him.

The violence of her thoughts and emotions shocked her. She was a pacifist. She'd attended anti-war demos, for cripes' sake!

She'd spent the past four months castigating herself for being stupid enough to fall for Pepe Mastrangelo's seduction. She should have known it wasn't her he was interested in. After all, he'd never displayed the slightest interest in her before. Not once.

On her frequent trips to Sicily to visit Grace, they would often make a foursome for evenings out. Luca had terrified her, had done from the moment she'd met him. Pepe, on the other hand, had been fun and charming. After a few dates she'd been able to converse with him as easily as she could with Grace. Tall and utterly gorgeous, he was the type of man females from all generations and all persuasions would pause to take a second look at.

However much she'd liked his irreverent company, she'd always known he tagged along on their evenings out as a favour to his big brother's wife. He would flirt with Cara as much as the next woman, fix his gorgeous dark blue eyes on her and make her feel as if she were the only woman in the world—until he fixed those same eyes on another woman and made her feel exactly the same way. His blatancy had made her laugh. It had also made her feel safe. He was not a man any woman with a sane mind could take seriously.

Well, more fool her for falling for it. She would *never* make the same mistake again, not for him, not for anyone.

Hadn't she always known that sex was nothing but a weapon? Hadn't she witnessed it with her own eyes, the devastation that occurred when grown men and women allowed their hormones to dictate their actions? It ripped lives and families apart.

Pepe was a man who positively revelled in allowing his hormones to lead the way. He thrived on it. To him, she, Cara, had been nothing but a means to an end, the sex between them a perk of the task he had undertaken. His brother had wanted his wife back and Cara's phone had contained the data with which to find her. The fact that she was a human being with real human feelings had meant nothing. When it came to his family, Pepe was a man without limits.

And that lack of limits had come at a price.

'I can't *"forget about it and move on"*, you feckless, irresponsible playboy, because I'm pregnant.'

CHAPTER TWO

CARA DIDN'T KNOW exactly how Pepe would react to her little statement, but when he finally turned to face her, his wide smile was still firmly in place.

'Is this your idea of a joke?'

'No. I'm sixteen weeks pregnant. Congratulations. You're going to be a daddy.'

His eyes bored into hers but his smile didn't dim, not by a single wattage. All around them gathered his family. She could feel their curious gazes resting on them. Resting on *her*.

It was too late to wish she could hide behind Grace as she had done so many times since her teenage years. Whenever she was in a new social situation she would let Grace hold court until her nerves were silenced and she felt capable of speaking without choking on her own tongue. Grace had understood. Grace had protected her.

But Grace had married and moved countries. Grace had also disappeared for the best part of a year, forcing Cara to get her own life in order. She couldn't keep living her life through her best friend. She needed a life that was her own.

And she'd been getting there. She'd moved back to Ireland, landed a job she loved, albeit at the lowest rung, but it was a start, and even made some new friends. She had truly thought she'd found her own path to some kind of fulfilling life.

Pepe hadn't just blocked the path, he'd driven a ruddy great bulldozer through it and churned it into rubble.

He'd left her alone, scared and pregnant, with a future that loomed terrifyingly opaque.

Eventually he inclined his head and nodded at the door. 'Come with me.'

Relieved to get away from all the prying eyes, relieved to have a moment to gather her wits together, she followed him out and into the wide corridor.

Pepe leaned against the stone wall and ran a hand through his thick black hair.

A maid appeared carrying a fresh tray of canapés, which she took into the vast living room.

No sooner had the maid gone when a couple of elderly uncles came out of the same door, laughing between themselves. When they saw Pepe, they pulled him in for some back-breaking hugs and fired a load of questions, all of which Pepe answered with gusto and laughter, as if he hadn't a single care in the world.

The minute they were alone though, the smile dropped. 'Let's get out of here before any more of my relatives try and talk to me.' He set off in a direction within the converted monastery she'd never been in before.

'Where are we going?'

'To my wing.'

He made no allowances for her legs being half the length of his, and she struggled to keep up. 'What for?'

He flashed her a black look over his shoulder, not slowing his pace for a moment. 'You really wish to have this conversation in front of fifty Mastrangelos and Lombardis?'

'Of course not, but I really don't want to have it in your personal space. Can't we go somewhere neutral?'

'No.' He stopped at a door, unlocked it and held it open. He extended an arm. 'I'm getting on a flight to Paris in exactly two hours. This is a one-off opportunity to convince me that I have impregnated you.'

She stared at him. She couldn't read his face. If anything, he looked bored. 'You think I'm lying?'

'You wouldn't be the first woman to lie over a pregnancy.'

Throwing him the most disdainful look she could muster, Cara slipped past him and into his inner sanctum.

Thank God she had no hankering for any sort of future for them. He was a despicable excuse for a human being.

Pepe's wing, although rarely used, what with him having at least three other places he called home, was exactly what she expected. Unlike the rest of the converted monastery, which remained faithful and sympathetic to the original architecture, this was a proper bachelor pad. It opened straight into a large living space decked with the largest flat-screen television she had seen outside a cinema, and was filled with more gizmos and gadgets than she'd known existed. She doubted she would know how to work a quarter of them.

She stood there, in the midst of all this high-tech luxury, and suddenly felt the first seed of doubt that she was doing the right thing.

'Can I get you a drink?'

'No. Let's just get this over with.' Of course she was doing the right thing, she castigated herself. Her unborn child deserved nothing less.

'Well, I need one.' He picked up a remote control from a glass table in the centre of the room and pressed a button.

Eyes wide, she watched as the oak panelling on the wall behind him separated and a fully stocked bar emerged.

Pepe mixed himself some concoction she didn't recognise. 'Are you sure I can't get you anything?'

'Yes.'

He tipped it down his neck and then fixed his deep blue eyes back to her. 'Go on, then. Convince me.'

Pursing her lips, she shook her head in distaste. 'I'm pregnant.'

'So you've already said.'

'That's because I am.'

'How much?'

'How much what?'

'Money. How much money are you going to try and extort from me?'

She glared at him. 'I'm not trying to extort anything from you.'

'So you don't want my money?' he said, his tone mocking.

'Of course I do.' It gave great satisfaction to watch his ebony brows shoot up. 'You have lots of money. I have nothing. I am broke. Boracic. Poor. Whatever you want to call it, I am skint. I'm also carrying a child whose father can afford to pay for a decent cot and wardrobe and a decent place for him or her to live.'

He sucked in air through his teeth. 'So you *are* trying to extort money from me.'

'No!' Clamping her lips together, Cara opened her handbag and took out a brown envelope, from which she pulled a square piece of paper. She handed it to him. 'There,' she said tightly. 'There's your proof. I'm not trying to extort anything from you. I'm sixteen weeks pregnant. You *are* going to be a father.'

For a moment Pepe feared he would be sick. His stomach was certainly churning enough for it to happen. And his skin…his skin had gone all cold and clammy; his heart rate tripled.

And no wonder.

If this were a forgery, Cara had done an excellent job.

The square piece of paper clearly showed a kidney bean. Or was it that alien thing he had watched as a child? E.T.? Either way, this was clearly an early-stage foetus. He studied it carefully. There was the name of the Dublin hospital on it, her name, Cara Mary Delaney, her date of birth and the due date of the foetus. He did the maths. Yes. This put her at sixteen weeks pregnant.

It had been sixteen weeks since he'd been to Dublin…

'You don't look very pregnant.' She looked thinner than he had ever seen her. She'd never been fat as such, more cuddly. While she hadn't transformed into a rake, she'd lost some of her, for want of a better word, *squishiness*.

'I've been under a lot of stress.' She gave him a tight smile. 'Unexpected pregnancy can do that to a woman. But the baby's perfectly healthy and I'm sure I'll start showing soon.'

He looked again at the scan picture. Cara was a smart woman but he doubted even she could forge something of this standard. The resolution on this picture was more clearly defined than the one he had held and gazed at for hours on end over a decade ago, but everything else was the same.

Cara was pregnant.

He looked back at her, realising for the first time that she was shaking. It took all his control to keep his own body still.

Dragging air into his lungs, he considered the situation as dispassionately as he could, which was hard. Very hard. His brain felt as if someone had thrown antifreeze into it. 'Congratulations. You're going to be a mother. Now tell me, what makes you so certain I'm the father?'

She opened her mouth, then closed it, then opened it again. 'What kind of stupid question is that? Of course you're the father. You're the only man I've been stupid enough to have sex with.'

'And I'm supposed to take your word on that, am I?'

'You know damn well I was a virgin.'

'I am not disputing that you were a virgin. What I am questioning is my paternity. I have no way of knowing what you got up to after I left. How do I know that after discovering all you'd been missing, you didn't go trawling for sex—?'

Her hand flew out from nowhere. *Crack.* Right across his cheek, the force enough to jerk his face to the side.

'Don't you dare pull me down to your own pathetically low standards,' she hissed, her face contorted with anger.

His cheek stung, smarted right where her hand and fingers had made contact. She might be small but she packed a proper punch. He could feel her imprint burrowing under his skin. He raised a hand to it. Her finger marks lay on the long scar that had been inflicted on him when he'd been eighteen. There were still times when he could feel the blade of the knife burn into his skin.

'I will let you do that this one time,' he said, speaking carefully, controlling his tone. 'But if you ever raise a hand to me again you will never see me or my money again.'

Her breaths were shallow. 'You deserved it.'

'Why? Because I pointed out that you are expecting me to take you at your word? Trust me, I take *no one* at their word, especially a woman purporting to be carrying my child.'

'I *am* carrying your child.'

'No—you are carrying *a* child. Until the child is born and we can get a paternity test done, I do not want to hear any reference to it being mine.' After what Luisa had done to him, he would never take anything to do with paternity at face value again. Never.

Only fools rushed in twice.

Cara itched to slap the arrogance off his face again, so much so that she dug her nails into the palms of her hands to find some relief.

If she could, she would leave. But she couldn't. She hadn't been exaggerating about the state of her bank balance. Paying for the return flight to Sicily had left her with the grand total of forty-eight euros to last her until payday, which was still a fortnight away. It was one thing living on baked beans on toast when she had only herself to support, but it was quite another when she would soon have a tiny mouth to feed and clothe. And she needed to find a new home, one that allowed children.

When she'd first discovered she was pregnant, her fear had been primitive, a cold, terrifying realisation that within her grew a life, a baby.

Jeez. A baby. She couldn't remember ever even *holding* a baby.

That real terror had morphed when the freeze in her brain had abated and the reality of everything that having a child meant had hit her.

A child would depend on her for *everything*. Love. Stability. Nourishment. Of the three, came the sharp knowledge that she would only be able to provide the first.

At that precise moment, even more so than when

she'd taken the pregnancy test, her life had changed irrevocably.

What stability did she have living in a shared rented home that banned children? What nourishment could she provide when she barely earned enough to feed herself? Nappies alone cost a fortune on her salary. Maybe if this had all happened a few years down the line, when she'd scaled the career ladder a little higher and was earning more, things would have been more manageable. But they weren't. At that moment she had nothing.

'So that's it, is it?' she demanded, fighting with everything she had to keep her tone moderate, to fight the hysteria threatening to take control. 'What do you want me to do? Give you a ring in five months and tell you if it's a boy or a girl?'

He speared her with a look. 'Not at all, *cucciola mia*.'

Cucciola mia: the endearment that had appropriated itself as his pet name for her during their weekend together. Curiosity had driven her to translate it on the same phone he had stolen from her. She had been more than a little chagrined to learn it meant something along the lines of *my puppy.* The way he said it though…in Pepe's thick Sicilian tongue it sounded tantalisingly sexy.

Momentarily distracted at the throwaway endearment, it took a second before she realised he was studying the scan picture.

'I notice this was taken a month ago,' he said, referring to the date of the scan shown clearly on the corner.

'And?'

'And it's taken you all this time to tell me. Why is that?'

How she hated his mocking scepticism, as if he were looking for a conspiracy in every little thing.

'I didn't tell you any sooner because I don't trust you

an inch—I wanted to be sure I was too far gone for you to force an abortion on me.'

Pepe's firm, sensuous lips tightened and his eyes narrowed, lines appearing on his forehead. After too long a pause, he said, 'Why would you think that?'

She almost laughed aloud. 'You have loved and left so many women it's become a second career for you. What do you, Playboy of the Year, want with a child?'

His features darkened for the split of a second before his usual laconic grin replaced it. 'It might make a nice accessory for pulling more women.'

She would have believed he was serious if the granite in his eyes hadn't said otherwise. She gave an involuntary shiver.

'Do you think I was oblivious to the disparaging comments you made about babies?' she demanded. 'Do you think I didn't notice you rolling your eyes whenever Grace and Luca discussed having kids?'

'So that's proof I would demand an abortion, is it?'

'You made it perfectly clear that kids are not and never will be on your agenda.'

A tiny pulse pounded on his jawline. After a loaded pause, he said, 'Say a paternity test proves it is mine. What do you expect from me? Marriage?'

'No!' She practically shouted her denial. 'No. I do not want to marry you. I don't want to marry anyone.'

'That's a relief,' he drawled, heading back to his bar to pour himself another glass of his concoction. 'But in case you're only saying what you think I want to hear, know marriage will never be on the cards, whatever the outcome of the paternity test.'

Had he drugged her? For a moment she actually considered the possibility. She could hardly credit she had allowed him to seduce her so thoroughly.

She looked back on their weekend together. It was as if she had been under some kind of drug that allowed the hormones so prevalent in the rest of society to actually work in her. For the first time in her life she had experienced desire. It had been the headiest feeling imaginable.

She had *wanted* to believe he was serious about her.

She had *wanted* to believe they could have a future together.

An image of her parents flashed in her head. Was this what it had been like for them? Especially her father, who'd hooked up with a new woman on a seemingly weekly basis. With all the affairs he'd had and all her parents' fights and making up, had they constantly experienced that same headiness? Was that what had caused their monstrous selfishness?

She blinked the image away. She would *not* be like her mother and think only of her own needs. Her unborn child's needs would always take priority, whatever the personal sacrifice.

'I'm glad you think that way because, believe me, I have no intention of marrying you.' She'd rather marry an orang-utan.

'Good. People who marry for the sake of the baby are fools. And I am not a fool.'

She glared at him. 'I can think of many a choice word to describe you but *fool* isn't one of them.'

'Then we are on the same page,' he mocked.

'About marriage, then yes, but, Pepe, I need help. Financially, I am in no position to support a child.'

'So you thought you would come to me.' He tipped his drink down his neck in one swallow.

'If you think for a second I like the idea of having to beg you for money then you have a very twisted view of me. I've come to you for help because this is your responsibility…'

'You're going to pin the blame for this on me?'

'I'm not the one who got carried away,' she countered pointedly. Warmth spread inside her as she recalled lying in his arms after they'd made love for the first time. Pepe's usual languidness had gone. A more serious, reflective side of his nature had come to the fore, a side she'd never seen before. As they'd talked and his face had come closer to hers, she'd found herself staring at his lips. And he'd been staring at hers. And even though they had made love barely ten minutes before, the heat he had created inside her and she in him had flared back to life, and he'd rolled on top of her and kissed her—devoured her—and before either of them had been fully aware of it, he'd been inside her. If she'd thought having him inside her the first time had been something special…this had been indescribable. For what had felt an age, they had simply lain there, gazing into each other's eyes, before he had reluctantly withdrawn to get a condom.

That one stolen moment had been enough to create a life.

'I hardly think that was enough to make a baby,' he said, his tone becoming grim.

'Well, it was. You used me, Pepe. Whether you like it or not, you are responsible.'

It sickened him to know she could be right.

You are responsible.

Despite the playboy image he had cultivated—an image he exulted in—Pepe couldn't remember the last time he'd been so reckless.

Actually, he could remember. The last time he'd made love to a woman without using a condom he'd been eighteen. Young and believing himself to be in love. A lethal combination.

It hadn't been a conscious decision to enter Cara unsheathed. At the time it had felt like the most natural thing in the world. Not that he'd been thinking properly. He'd been reeling from the discovery that she was—had been—a virgin. He'd also been struggling to understand everything going on inside *him*.

Usually he would make love to a woman and get back into bed, have a fun conversation, drink a glass of wine or whatever, maybe make love again and then leave without a second thought or a backward glance. He'd never got back into bed with a churning stomach and a tight chest before. He could only assume it was guilt he'd been feeling. Guilt at her virginity or guilt at what he'd had to do, he did not know.

Guilt or not, he'd *never* got back into bed with a woman and needed to make love to her all over again. Not straight away. For all his reputation, Pepe thought with his brain, not the appendage between his legs. At least he had until that night with Cara.

But he hadn't been inside her for long enough to make a baby. It had been a minute at the most. But *caro Dio*, he'd had to force himself to withdraw and get that condom. Being inside her without a barrier…

His groin twitched as more sweet memories filled him.

For that one minute inside her, he'd felt a sense of sheer wonderment and belonging…

'I need a coffee,' he muttered. He wanted another drink—a proper drink—but knew it was time to stop. A plan was formulating and he needed to think clearly. 'Can I get you anything?'

Cara shook her head. She was leaning against the wall, arms folded, chin jutted up, looking ready for a fight.

By the time he'd made a quick call to the kitchen, his plan was fully developed. Cara could like it or lump it. If she wanted a fight, she had to learn it was one she would never win.

CHAPTER THREE

'SIT DOWN.'

It was a definite command.

Cara tightened her arms around her chest and pressed harder into the wall, which was the only thing keeping her upright—her legs were shot. Not that she could trust the wall. For all she knew, it might be hiding a secret bathroom. The only saving grace was that her dress was long enough to hide her knocking knees.

But even if her legs could be trusted to behave, there was no way she would obey. She didn't care how rich and powerful Pepe was in his world, she would not grant him power over her, no matter how petty. Not without a fight.

'Suit yourself.' He lowered himself onto one of the oversized chocolate leather sofas, stretched out his long legs, kicked off his shoes and flashed a grin.

Her knees shook even harder.

How she hated that bloody grin. It was so...fake. And it did something ridiculous to the beat of her heart, which was hammering so hard she wouldn't be in the least surprised if it burst through her chest.

'I can see you are in a difficult predicament,' he said, hooking an arm behind his head and mussing his hair.

She inhaled slowly, getting as much oxygen into her lungs as she could. 'That's one way to describe it.'

'I have a solution that will suit us both.'

Her eyes narrowed.

'It involves sacrifice on both our parts.' He shot her a warning glance before displaying his white teeth. 'But I can assure you that if I am the father of your child as you say, the sacrifice will be worth it.'

What the heck did Pepe Mastrangelo know about sacrifice? His whole life revolved around nothing but his pleasure.

She nodded tightly. 'Go on.'

'You will live with me until the child is born. Then we shall have a paternity test. If it proves positive, as you say it will, then I will buy you a home of your choice. And, of course, support you both financially.'

'You want me to live with you until the baby's born?' she asked, certain she had misheard him.

'Sì.'

'Why?' She couldn't think of a single reason. 'All I need from you at the moment is enough money to rent a decent flat in a nice area, and buy some essentials for the baby. Obviously you'll have to pay child support when the baby's born.'

'Only if the baby proves to be mine. If it isn't, I won't have to pay you a single euro.'

Cara spoke through gritted teeth. 'The baby is yours. But seeing as you're proving to be such a disbeliever, I'm happy to sign a contract stating I have to repay any monies in the event the paternity test proves the Invisible Man is the father.'

He gave a quick shake of his head and turned his mouth down in a regretful fashion. 'If only it were that simple. The problem, for me, is that there exists the possibility that the child you carry inside you *is* mine. I cannot take the risk of anything happening to it.'

'I told you I delayed telling you about the baby so you couldn't force me into an abortion. I'm four weeks too late for one in Sicily and it's completely illegal in Ireland.' She blinked rapidly, fighting with everything she had not to burst into angry tears. She would not give him the satisfaction of seeing her cry. She would not give him the power her mother had given her father.

She might have no choice but to throw her pride at his feet but she had to retain some kind of dignity.

'I never said anything about an abortion,' he pointed out. 'What does concern me is your health. You're clearly not taking care of yourself if your weight loss is anything to go by, and by your own admittance you don't have enough money to support a child. Or so you say. For all I know, you could be on the make, using this pregnancy as a means to help yourself to my bank account.'

It was Cara's turn to swear under her breath. 'Do you have any idea how offensive you are?'

He shrugged, utterly nonchalant. He clearly couldn't care less. 'Finances aside, if that *is* my child growing inside you then I want to make damned sure you're taking care of it properly.'

'I am taking care of myself as best I can under the circumstances, but, I can promise you, our child's welfare means more to me than anything.' Her unborn child meant *everything* to her. Everything. Its well-being was the only reason she was here.

Did Pepe think she *wanted* to throw herself at his financial mercy?

He shook his head in a chiding fashion and stretched his arms out. 'My conditions are non-negotiable. If you want me to support you during the rest of the pregnancy then I will. But I will not give you cash. All you have to do is move in with me, travel where I travel, and I will feed and clothe you, and buy anything else you may need. If paternity is established after the birth, then I will buy you a house in your name, anywhere you choose, and give you an allowance so large you will be set up for life.'

He made it sound so reasonable. He made it sound as if it were such a no-brainer she wouldn't even need to think about it.

And there she'd been, worrying for months against telling him because she'd convinced herself he would demand an abortion.

'You see, *cucciola mia*, I am not the baby-aborting monster you thought I would be,' he said chidingly, reading her mind.

A sharp rap on the main door to the wing provided a moment's relief for her poor, addled brain.

At Pepe's invitation, a maid entered the room carrying a tray with a pot of coffee, a pot of tea covered by a tea cosy and two cups.

'It's decaf,' he explained when it had been placed on the glass table and the maid left.

'I told you I didn't want anything.'

'You need to keep your fluid levels up.'

'Oh, so you're a doctor now? Or have you an army of illegitimates scattered around the world that's made you a pregnancy expert?'

He quelled her with a glance.

She refused to bow to its latent warning. 'Sorry. Am I supposed to believe this is the first time you've had a paternity suit thrown at you?'

His eyes were unreadable. 'I always use protection.'

'And you're expecting me to take you at your word for that?'

His features darkened before his lips gave a slight twitch and he bowed his head. 'A fair comeback.'

He really was ridiculously handsome.

She castigated herself. As far as she was concerned, Pepe's looks and masculinity were void. She would *not* let her hormones create any more havoc.

It was unfair that she was the one standing yet it still felt as if he, all chilled and relaxed on the sofa, had all the advantage.

A whorl of black hair poked through the top of his shirt. She remembered how that same hair covered his chest, thickening across his tightly defined pecs and down the middle towards his navel, and further down... She'd always assumed chest hair would be bristly, had been thrilled to find it as soft as silk. It was the only thing soft about him; everything else was hard...

She swallowed and pressed the tops of her thighs together to try to quash the heat bubbling within her.

Her throat had gone dry.

Damn him, she needed a drink.

Lips clamped together, she moved away from the wall and poured herself a cup of the steaming tea before carrying it to the sofa opposite him. She only intended to perch there but it was so soft and squidgy it almost swallowed her whole. She sank straight into it, her legs shooting out, the motion causing her to spill the tea all over her lap.

Cara cried out, kicking her legs as if the movement would stop the hot fluid seeping through her dress.

Immediately Pepe jumped to his feet and hurried over, snatching the cup from her hand. 'Are you okay?'

In too much pain to do anything more than whimper, Cara grabbed the hem of her dress and bunched it up to her thighs, flapping it to cool her heated skin. Making sure to keep the dress up and away from the scald, she yanked the tops of her black hold-ups down.

'Are you okay?' he repeated. For some silly reason,

the genuine concern she heard in his voice bothered her far more than the scald.

The milky white of her left thigh had turned a deep pink, as had a couple of patches on her right thigh. She took a deep breath. 'It hurts.'

'I'll bet. Can you walk?'

'Why?'

'Because we should run cold water over it.'

Her thighs—especially her left one—were stinging something rotten, so much so she didn't even think of arguing with him.

'Come, we'll run the shower on it.'

Wincing, she let him help her to her feet.

Her legs shook frantically enough that she almost fell back onto the sofa, only Pepe's grip on her hand keeping her upright.

He frowned and shook his head, then, before she knew what he was doing, lifted her into his arms, taking great care not to touch her thighs.

'This is unnecessary,' she complained. She might be in pain but she didn't need *this*. Besides, she was vain enough to know she must look ridiculous with her dress bunched around the tops of her thighs, her modesty barely preserved. Her stupid black hold-ups had fallen down to her knees like the socks of a scatty schoolgirl.

'Probably,' he agreed, heading through the living area and into a narrow corridor, carrying her as if she weighed little more than a child. 'But it's quicker and safer than you trying to walk.'

The position he held her in meant her face was right in the crook of his strong, bronzed neck. A compulsion to press her face into it almost overcame her. Almost. Luckily she still retained some control. But she'd forgotten how delicious he smelt, like sun-ripened fruit. Her position meant her senses were filled with it and she had to use even more restraint not to lick him.

Pepe's bathroom was twice the size of her bedroom and resembled a miniature black, white and gold palace. She had no time to appreciate its splendour.

'You're going to have to take your dress off,' he said as he carried her down some marble steps and carefully sat her on the edge of the sunken bath.

'I jolly well am not.'

'It will get wet.'

'It's already wet.'

'Suit yourself.' He knelt before her and placed a hand on her knee.

She tried not to yelp. 'What are you doing?'

'Taking your stockings off.' He tugged the first one down to the ankle. While she hated herself for her vanity, Cara could not help feel relief that she'd remembered to wax her legs a few days ago.

'They're hold-ups,' she corrected, breathing deeply. The trail of his fingers on her skin burned almost as much as the scald.

'They're sexy.'

'That's inappropriate.'

His lips twitched. 'Sorry.'

'Liar.'

Hold-ups removed and thrown onto the floor, Pepe helped manoeuvre her into the empty bath before reaching for the shower head that rested on the gold taps.

He held it over his hand then turned it on. Water gushed out, spraying over them both.

Adjusting the pressure, he smiled with a hint of smugness. 'Still happy to keep your dress on?'

'Yes.' She would rather suffer third-degree burns than strip off to her underwear in front of him.

'I've seen you naked before,' he reminded her wickedly, turning the shower onto her thighs.

'Not under bright light, you haven't.'

The cold water felt like the greatest relief in the world. Cara closed her eyes, rested her head back and savoured the feeling, uncaring that the cold water spraying off her thighs was pooling in the base of the bath, sloshing all around her bottom. It was worth it. Slowly, wonderfully, her tender skin numbed.

It was only when she opened her eyes a few minutes later that she realised her dress had risen higher and that her black knickers were fully exposed.

One look at the gleam in Pepe's eyes and she knew he'd noticed.

'I think that's enough now,' she said, leaning up and yanking her sodden dress down to cover herself.

Pepe screwed his eyes shut to rid himself of the image.

It didn't work.

The image of Cara's soaking knickers and the memories of what they hid burned brightly, almost as brightly as her flushing cheeks.

His trousers felt so tight and uncomfortable it was hard to breathe.

He gritted his teeth and willed his erection to abate.

He turned the tap off, replaced the shower head and crouched back next to her, making sure to look at her face and only her face. 'Your thighs should be okay—it doesn't look as if they're going to blister—but to play safe I've got some salve in the medicine cabinet you can put on them. I'll get it for you and then you can get changed— where's your change of clothes?'

'I didn't bring any.'

'Why not?' Whenever Cara came to Sicily she always came for at least a week.

'I only came for the day.'

'Really?' He'd arrived from Paris with barely twenty minutes to spare before the christening started, avoiding the inevitable for as long as humanly possible. He hadn't imagined Cara had done the same.

'I didn't want to risk spilling the beans to Grace before I'd had a chance to speak to you.'

'That was good of you,' he acknowledged.

'Not really.' Her face tightened. 'I was worried she'd be unable to keep it from Luca and that Luca in turn would tell you.'

Upon reflection, Pepe was certain that if his sister-in-law had known she would have tracked him down at the earliest opportunity and given him hell. 'I'll ask Grace if she has any clothes you can borrow...'

'You jolly well won't.' Cara glared at him.

'You're right. Bad idea.' If he sought Grace out he'd have to explain why her best friend was sitting with scalded thighs in his bath, and then everything about the baby would become common knowledge... 'Have you told *anyone* about the baby?'

'Only my mother, but she doesn't count.'

'Good,' he said, ignoring the tightening of her lips as she mentioned her mother. He had enough to think about as it was.

'Why's that, then? Worried all those doting Mastrangelo aunts and uncles will try and marry us off?'

'They can try all they like,' he answered with a shrug. Given a chance, they'd have him and Cara up the aisle quicker than it had taken to impregnate her.

That was if he *had* impregnated her.

He didn't care that she'd been a virgin, he didn't care that the dates tallied—until he saw cast-iron proof of his paternity he would not allow himself to believe anything. 'I bow to no one.'

'Well, neither do I. Your suggestion that I move in with you is ridiculous. How the heck would I be able to get to and from work if I have to travel all over the place with you? You work all over Europe.'

'And South America,' he pointed out. 'You'll have to give up your job.'

He noticed her shiver and remembered she'd just had a cold shower pressed against her for the best part of ten minutes.

'Let's get you out of the bath. We can finish this argument when you're dry and warm.'

'I'm not giving up my job and I'm not moving in with you.'

'I said we can argue the toss when you're dry.'

He could see how much she hated having to use him for support. Not looking at him, she allowed him to help her to her feet. He held her arms and kept her steady while she climbed out of the bath.

She looked like a drowned rat. Even her face was soaked.

Too late, he realised it was tears rolling down her cheeks.

'You're crying?'

'I'm crying because I'm angry,' she sobbed. 'You've ruined my life and now you want to ruin my future too. I *hate* you.'

He took a large, warm towel off the rack and wrapped it around her shaking frame before taking a deliberate step back. 'If you're telling me the truth then your future is made. I'll give you and the baby more money than you could ever hope to spend.'

'I don't want to be a kept woman. I just want what *our* child is entitled to.'

'You won't have to be a kept woman. The option will be there for you, that's all. If your child is mine, you'll have enough money to do whatever you want. You can hire a nanny—hell, you'll be able to hire an army of them—and return to work.'

Her teeth clattered together. 'But I won't have a job to go back to.'

'There are other jobs.'

'Not like this one. Do you have any idea how hard it is getting a foot on the ladder in the art world without *any* contacts?'

'There are other jobs,' he repeated. Deep inside his chest, a part of him had twisted into a tight ball, but he ignored it. He had to. He could not allow any softening towards her, no matter how vulnerable she looked at that particular moment.

Luisa had shown her vulnerable side numerous times. It had all been a big fat lie and he had been the sucker who had fallen for it. Every day he looked in the mirror and saw the evidence of her lies reflecting back at him. He could have had surgery to remove his scar. Instead he had chosen to keep it as a reminder not to trust and, more especially, not to love.

'You don't have to move in with me,' he said. He drew the towel together so it covered her more thoroughly and forced himself to stare into her damp eyes. He refused to break the hold, no matter the misery reflecting back at him. 'You can catch your flight back to Ireland and carry on eking out an existence. Or you can stay. If you stay, I will support you and we can take the paternity test as soon as the child is born. But if you leave now, you will not receive a single euro from me until my paternity—or lack of it—has been proven. And if you choose to leave, you'll have to go through the courts to get a DNA sample from me. That's if you can find me. As you know, I have homes in four different countries. I can make it extremely difficult for you to get that sample.'

He knew how unreasonable he must sound but he didn't care.

He could not afford to allow himself to care.

If Cara really was carrying his child then he must make every effort to protect its innocent form, and the only way he could do that was by forcing her into a corner from which the only means of escape was his way. Short of tying her up and locking her in a windowless room, this was his best chance of keeping her by his side until the birth.

He would not risk losing another child.

CHAPTER FOUR

CARA DIDN'T THINK she'd ever felt as self-conscious as she did at that moment, and she'd had plenty of experience of feeling awkward and insecure.

Pepe's blue shirt came to her knees and she'd rolled his trousers over so many times to get them to fit lengthways that it looked as if she had two wedges around her ankles. All she needed was a pair of extra-long shoes and she'd make the perfect clown.

Following him up the metal steps and into his jet, she forced herself to return the smiles and friendly greetings given by the glamorous cabin crew. Not one of them batted an eyelid at her presence. Most likely because strange women accompanying Pepe on his travels was par for the course, she thought snidely.

The jet was a proper flying bachelor pad, all leather and dark hardwood panelling. A steward showed her to a seat for take-off. She was nonplussed when Pepe took the seat next to her.

'You have ten seats to choose from,' she said, glaring at him.

'So do you,' he pointed out in return, strapping himself in and stretching his long legs out. He looked at the cheap mobile phone in her hand. 'Who are you contacting?'

'Grace.'

'What are you going to say to her?'

'That her brother-in-law is a feckless scumbag with the morals of an amoeba.'

He cocked an eyebrow.

She sighed. 'I wanted to write that but until we've got the finances sorted I'm not prepared to risk her ripping your head off.'

'That's decent of you,' he said drily.

She speared him with another poisonous glare then hit send. 'I've apologised for leaving the christening without saying goodbye. I've also told her I cadged a lift off you to the airport. Someone was bound to have seen us leave together.'

'Are you worried people will talk?' Pepe didn't sound worried. If anything, he sounded bored.

'Nope.' Let them think what they liked. The truth would come out. It always did. And when the truth came out, people would see that, beneath the charming, affable exterior, Pepe Mastrangelo was a horrid specimen of a man. 'I don't want Grace worrying, that's all.'

It crossed her mind, not for the first time, that she should have gone to Grace for help. In normal circumstances Cara *would* have gone to Grace, but when she'd found out she was pregnant, Grace had been in hiding, going through her own troubles. So, she'd told her mother, but her mam was going through yet another of her new husband's infidelities and so hadn't been particularly interested other than on a superficial level. Not that Cara had expected anything else from the woman who had given birth to her.

But then Luca had tracked Grace down and now the pair of them were madly in love and in a bubble of happiness. It would have been the perfect opportunity to ask for help.

Grace would have given her money and anything else she needed, no questions asked. But Cara wouldn't have been able to keep it contained and the whole sordid story would have come out, and then God knew what would have happened.

In any case, her child was not her friend's responsibility. It was Pepe's.

And this mess was not of Grace's making. This was all on her, Cara. And the feckless playboy, of course.

It was too late to go to Grace for help now. Pepe would undoubtedly turn to Luca, who in turn would put pressure on his wife not to give Cara any financial help. Grace was so loved up at the moment she would probably comply. At the very least it would cause friction between them.

Thanks to Pepe, she couldn't turn to the one person she needed.

The steward, who was still making checks and pretending not to listen to their conversation, finally disappeared into a separate cabin.

'How are your thighs?' Pepe asked. If he was fazed about anything, he had yet to show it.

'Not too bad.' The salve he had given her had been bliss to apply. He'd also given her a wrap that resembled cling film to place on it too. He'd been so... *Concerned* was the wrong word but it was the closest for the way he'd treated her wounds. Not that he'd treated *her* with the same consideration.

How could someone be so gentle and at the same time be so horribly uncaring? That was part of what had tipped her over the edge and set the waterworks off.

'You should take the trousers off. I'm sure it can't help with the material rubbing against it.'

'They're fine.' No way was she taking any of her clothes off within a ten-mile radius of him ever again.

The plane began to taxi down the runway. Cara turned to look out of the window, a lump forming in her throat.

This was utter madness.

'Pepe, please, let me return to Dublin, just for a couple of days to get things in order.' It was an argument they'd had three times in the past hour.

'Impossible. I have a full day of business tomorrow and a business dinner in the evening.'

'Yes, but I don't. I'm supposed to be at work!'

'You will attend my meeting with me.'

She took a deep breath. Her blood pressure really didn't need any more aggravation.

'As I have made you more than aware, the week ahead is filled with appointments.'

'I have to wait until the weekend to go back home?' she said, horror-struck.

'I'm afraid a trip back to Dublin is not on the schedule for the foreseeable future.'

'You're kidding me?'

'You can make any necessary arrangements via other means.'

'So I have to hand in my notice by text or email?'

He shrugged. 'It's entirely up to you how you want to handle it.'

'I'd like to handle it by *not* giving up my job,' she stated angrily. 'But seeing as I *do* have to quit, I'd prefer to tell my boss in person.'

He almost looked sympathetic. 'I appreciate this is an inconvenience but if, as you say, the baby is mine, you will be well recompensed for any aggravation.'

'And my housemates? Will they be *recompensed* too?'

His brow furrowed.

'I'm leaving them in the lurch. If you won't let me go

to Dublin, I can't clear my room out and they can't find another housemate to take my place.'

'That is not a problem. I can send someone over to clear your room for you.'

'You will not!' There was no way she wanted some stranger rifling through her knicker drawer. Closing her eyes, she slowly expelled a lungful of air. They had been so busy arguing she'd barely noticed the jet increase in speed. Suddenly her stomach lurched and she was leaning back.

The jet became airborne.

She took another deep breath. 'If I contact my housemates and ask them to get all my stuff together, can you send someone to collect it?'

'Of course.'

'Can they get it to me for tomorrow morning?'

'Why so soon?'

'Because I have nothing on me apart from my handbag and a stick of mascara. I need my stuff.'

'I've already made arrangements for new clothing to be delivered to the house first thing for you.'

Of course he had. For such a languid person Pepe was proving surprisingly efficient.

'I want *my* stuff.'

'And you will have it. Soon.'

'How soon?'

'Soon. And I will ensure your housemates get adequate compensation from your missed rent.'

'Good.' She would not say thank you.

Her stomach rolled again and she breathed in deeply through her nose.

'Are you okay?'

She did *not* want to hear any concern from him. 'I'm pregnant. My child's father is refusing to acknowledge paternity without a blood test yet still thinks it's acceptable to make me give up my job—a job I love—and leave my housemates in the doodle to follow him around the world like some sort of concubine. Plus I have no clothing or toiletries on me. So, yes. Everything is dandy.'

His gorgeous blue eyes darkened further and crinkled with amusement. 'My concubine, eh? Do you know what a concubine is?'

She felt her cheeks go scarlet. 'It was a statement of my unhappiness not a statement of fact.'

'A concubine is, in essence, a man's mistress.'

'I'm well aware of that.'

'A man pays for all his concubine's bills, buys property for her—'

'Basically a concubine is there for a man's pleasure when he's bored of his wife's company,' she interrupted. 'But seeing as you have no wife, I can't be your concubine.'

A gleam came into his eyes. 'Ah, so as I have no wife, does that mean you are going to be the main source of my pleasure?'

'I'd rather eat worms.'

'I'm sure I can think of something better for you to e—'

'Don't go there. I feel sick enough as it is.'

He laughed. 'That's not how I remember things.'

'Watch it or I will vomit.' But not through the memories of their night together.

Those memories moved her in wholly different ways.

Nope, the queasiness in her belly was solely due to motion sickness. She scrunched her eyes closed and took a long deep breath.

Pepe twisted onto his side to stare at her. Cara really

was incredibly sexy, even with her face contorted into a grimace.

But he would not go there again. Flirting with her was just asking for trouble. They had enough problems to get through.

She opened one eye. 'What?'

'Sorry?'

'You're staring at me.'

'Can't a man stare at a gorgeous woman?' Okay, so flirting was asking for trouble, but Cara really did look beautiful when she was angry, as clichéd as he knew that was.

'I'm pregnant,' she spat.

'You're also incredibly sexy. A man would have to be dead from the waist down not to desire you. But have no fear—I'm not going to make any unwanted passes at you.' All the same, he felt a tightening in his groin and almost groaned aloud at the incongruity of it all.

Cara despised him. No matter how much he might still desire her and, he suspected, she still desired him, he preferred his women to not loathe the very sound of his name.

And sex between them…nothing good could come of it. It had got him into enough trouble as it was, just as he'd always suspected sex with Cara would—why else had he kept such a distance from her sexually before?

In the world in which he mixed, sex was freely given with no real commitment assumed by anyone. Pepe liked it that way. It saved messy entanglements and even messier goodbyes. Everyone knew where they stood, no one got hurt, and everyone was happy.

'Well, that's good to know,' Cara said sarcastically. 'Let me guess—now that you don't need anything from me, there's no need to pretend any more.'

'What do you mean?'

'You never desired me before you needed to get hold of my phone.'

'On the contrary, *cucciola mia*, I've always found you incredibly attractive.'

'I'm pretty sure you find any woman with a pulse attractive. I'm saying you never desired *me* in particular.'

'I did, but I'm terrified of my sister-in-law. She would have tied me naked to a tree if I'd tried anything on with you.'

Despite herself, Cara snickered. Pepe was the cause of all her stress yet somehow he was able to soothe much of it away. The git. 'I would have loved to have seen that.'

'Don't worry—if the baby does turn out to be mine then I'm sure you'll get your chance when Grace finds out.'

'There's no *if* about it. This baby is yours.'

'Time will tell.' A black eyebrow shot up, a quizzical groove appearing in his forehead. 'If it *is* my child, will I also have to worry about your angry father beating at my door?'

'Seeing as he's not around, that's the last thing you'll have to worry about.'

He straightened in his seat, consternation replacing his amusement. 'Oh. I'm sorry. I didn't realise you'd lost your father too.'

It occurred to her that this was the closest Pepe had come to showing genuine contrition all day.

'My father isn't dead,' she quickly clarified, recalling being told his own father had died over a decade ago.

He looked confused. 'Then surely he will want to rip my head off and play football with it?'

She couldn't help the wry smile that formed on her lips, although she experienced the usual sickening churn in her belly she felt whenever she thought of her father. 'I'm sure there's a lot of fathers out there who would love nothing more than to cause you actual bodily harm, but I can assure you my dad's not one of them.'

'Why not? A father's job is to look out for his child.'

'My dad never bothered to read the job description.' Only years of faux nonchalance on the subject kept the bitterness from her voice, yet the churning increased, a situation not helped by the roils in her belly from the motion of the jet. Talking about her father always made her feel so *raw*. 'Believe me, if he were to meet you, the closest he would come to touching you is putting a hand on your shoulder and insisting on buying you a beer.'

For all of Pepe's antics and reputation, he knew damn well that if he had a daughter and some man lied to her and impregnated her, then he would certainly want to rip that man's head off.

Not that he was admitting to having impregnated Cara. Not yet. Not until the DNA test proved it beyond any doubt. And until that DNA test proved it, he would not allow himself to think of that child as being anything but a foetus. After what Luisa had put him through, this was an essential act of self-preservation.

He thought back to a time over a decade before when he had been looking at a scan of a foetus, trying to discern a head and tiny limbs from what was little more than a kidney bean. The emotions provoked by looking at that scan were the strongest he had ever experienced. Totally overwhelming. He had felt fit to burst. He could only imagine the strength of his feelings if that little life had been allowed to develop and allowed to be born.

But that little life had *not* been allowed to develop and be born, a fact that resided inside his guts like a vat of poison...

All the same, he could not imagine having a child and being so disassociated from their feelings that he didn't care if they were used and hurt. He might only be the 'spare' of the family, but he had never doubted his parents' love for him.

It was their respect he'd always failed to achieve.

He could well imagine how his brother would react if anyone were to hurt Lily. That person would likely never walk again.

Cara must have seen the way his thoughts were going because her features contorted into a grimace. 'Do you know, now I think about it, you and my father are incredibly alike. He's a charmer, just like you. Maybe I should introduce you to him—you can exchange shagging tips.'

It took every muscle in his face to keep his smile fixed there. 'Why do I feel I have just been insulted?'

'Because you're not as stupid as you look?' Before he could react to this latest insult, she stood up. 'If it's all the same to you, I'm going to curl up on that sofa and get some sleep. I assume one of the stewards will wake me before we land?'

She *did* look tired. So tired he bit back any further retort and any further questions about her father. Like it or not, she was pregnant and, now that he'd admitted her into his life, her health was his responsibility. Her already pale face was drained of colour.

He experienced a twinge that could be interpreted as concern. 'Are you feeling all right? Physically, I mean,' he added before she could bombard him with another long list of all the wrongs he had done.

'I'm feeling a little icky. But don't worry—it's not bad enough that you have to worry for your upholstery.'

He watched as she made her way to the sofa, holding on to something fixed for stability with every step.

A tap on the door broke through Cara's slumber.

There was none of that 'where am I' malarkey often

experienced when awaking under a new roof. Before she even opened her eyes she knew exactly where she was.

Pepe's house. Or, to be more precise, in a guest room in Pepe's Parisian house.

She'd pretended to sleep for the rest of the flight back to Charles de Gaulle airport. It certainly beat talking to him.

She'd ignored him as they'd gone through Customs, blanked him on the drive back to his house and pretended to be deaf when they arrived at his home, a five-storey town house in an exclusive Parisian suburb. She'd also pretended to be mute. She'd had to clamp her lips so tightly together when she was shown to her room that she'd pretended they'd been superglued. It was either that or have him witness her wonder at its sheer beauty. For a house purported to have been bought to show-case Pepe's art collection—and it was every bit as huge and glamorous as she'd expected—it had a surprisingly homely charm to it.

But she wouldn't tell Pepe that. She didn't want him to think she liked anything about him, not even his beautiful home.

It was talking about her father that had done it.

Her father, the arch charmer, the man who could make a woman forgive him over and over, make a woman believe his faults were in fact *her* faults.

Pepe's charm had always felt different from her father's. He had none of her father's seediness. Or sleaze.

But one thing he did have was the ability to make her *want* to believe in him. She'd wanted to believe Pepe saw her as more than a one-night stand. On his jet she'd felt herself thawing towards him, his gorgeous, easy-going smile slowly melting the edge of her defences. More than that, though, had been the unexpected depths she'd seen in his eyes. For a few moments she could have sworn she'd seen pain in them, something dark, something that hinted there was more to him than what he wore on the surface.

She'd thought she'd seen more to him that weekend in Dublin when he had seduced her so thoroughly. And it had all been a lie. Just as everything that came out of her father's mouth was a lie.

Pepe was of the same mould. Something she would do well to remember.

She sat up and rubbed her eyes.

Another knock at the door.

'Mademoiselle Delaney?' came a muffled female voice.

'I'm awake,' she called back, slipping out of the bed. Much as she hated to admit it, that had to qualify as *the* most comfortable bed she had ever slept on.

The handle turned and a middle-aged woman carrying a tray of coffee and croissants walked in.

Cara remembered her from their arrival, was certain Pepe had introduced her as Monique, his housekeeper.

'Good morning,' said Monique, heading straight for a small round table in the corner of the room and placing the tray on it. 'Did you sleep well?'

'Yes, thank you,' she answered in a small voice, forcing a smile. She always felt so…*noodley* when with strangers, as if her tongue had loosened, then tied itself into knots.

'Your deliveries have arrived,' Monique told her, drawing back the heavy full-length curtains to reveal a small balcony.

Morning sunshine filled the room.

Cara cleared her throat. 'What deliveries?'

'From the boutiques. I will bring them to you now.

Monsieur Mastrangelo has requested that you be ready to leave in an hour.'

Her heart sinking, Cara remembered a trip to the Loire Valley was on the day's agenda.

Her spirits lifted a fraction when Monique, assisted by a young woman, brought the boxes of clothes in to her, and a hand-case of toiletries.

'If there is anything else you require, please let me know,' Monique said before leaving the room.

Putting her half-eaten croissant to one side, Cara began going through the boxes, her spirits sinking all over again as she fingered the beautiful fabrics and accessories.

Why couldn't Pepe have ensured the clothing he'd ordered for her was inappropriate and gross? Here was an entire wardrobe for her and there was not a single item she wouldn't have selected herself if money had not been an object. Simple, elegant, casual clothing with an innate vibrancy. Even the nightdresses he'd ordered were beautiful.

When she opened the hand-case she wanted to scream with both joy and despair. Enclosed was every lotion and potion a woman could want, and make-up selected especially for her colouring. Worst of all was that it was all brands she coveted. She would walk past their counters in department stores and gaze at the beautiful items, promising herself that she would buy them when she earned enough money.

Shouldn't she be pleased she had them roughly five years ahead of schedule? Maybe she should but she couldn't muster up the necessary sparkly feelings. She didn't want to feel any gratitude towards Pepe. Wasn't that how Stockholm syndrome started? Not that she'd been kidnapped, not in the traditional sense of the word.

In the 'really not been given any other option' sense of the word then she had been.

She gathered all the toiletries together and took them into the en suite. Before stepping into the shower, she examined her thighs. Pepe's ointment was a marvel. The only discernible sign of injury was a slight pink mark. No pain *at all*.

The shower itself invigorated her. The gel smelt so utterly gorgeous and the water pressure and heat were so marvellous that she washed herself twice.

Well, that certainly beat the pathetic excuse for a shower she had in her shared bathroom in Dublin.

Wrapping a large fluffy white towel securely around her, she wandered back into her bedroom. She needed to select something to wear, which in theory shouldn't be a problem, but when one was confronted with a dozen beautiful outfits it became one.

For the first time in her life she had a problem selecting what to wear.

Just as she'd decided on a pair of designer black jeans and a cherry-red cashmere jumper, there was another knock on her door.

'Come in,' she called, expecting to see Monique standing there.

Her welcoming smile turned into a scowl when she found Pepe there instead.

CHAPTER FIVE

'WHAT DO YOU WANT?'

'Good morning to you too, *cucciola mia*,' he replied with a flash of his straight white teeth. He was wearing a grey suit with a white shirt and a black cravat. Yes. A cravat. Pepe wore a cravat that should look ridiculous but instead…

He looked far too gorgeous for sensibility.

'We need to leave shortly.'

Cara shrugged. 'If you want me to come with you, then you'll have to wait. I'm not ready.'

'Monique told you to be ready in an hour. That was an hour ago.'

'I don't wear a watch and my phone's out of battery, so I have no way of knowing what the time is. I would charge my phone but the charger's in Dublin,' she added pointedly.

'Is no problem,' he said, brushing his way past her and perching on her bed. 'As you suggested, I will wait for you.'

'Not in here, you won't.'

'And you are going to stop me how?' he asked in a chiding fashion.

She speared him with the nastiest glare she could muster.

He laughed softly, which made her scowl all the more.

Still laughing, he rummaged through one of the boxes and held up a pair of skimpy black lace knickers. 'Are you going to wear these?'

She snatched them from him, knowing her cheeks had turned a deep red to match her hair. 'Get out and let me get changed.'

'I would but I have a feeling you will get ready quicker if I'm in here with you.'

Calling him every nasty word she knew under her breath but loud enough for him to hear, Cara gathered her selected outfit and swept off back into the en suite, letting the door shut with a bang.

For a moment she was reluctant to take the towel off. She had no fear he would barge in on her—where that certainty came from, she could not say—but it wouldn't surprise her in the least to learn he had X-ray vision.

The thought made her feel distinctly off-kilter, in a way that was completely inappropriate.

The thought of Pepe staring at her naked body while she was oblivious should *not* make her breasts feel heavy...

Swallowing away moisture that had suddenly filled her mouth, she pulled her knickers on, too late recalling them being the same pair Pepe had just fingered.

This was how he'd been able to seduce her so easily.

For some reason her testosterone-immune body re-acted to Pepe and became pathetic and weak-willed around him.

By the end of their weekend together she had been like a lust-filled nympho.

What was it about him?

And what was so wrong with her that she still reacted to him, even after everything he had done? Not forgetting that she was pregnant—shouldn't pregnancy act as a natural form of anti-aphrodisiac? If it didn't, it jolly well should.

Pathetic. That's what she was.

Dressed, she went back into the room. Pepe had moved to an armchair in the corner, his long legs stretched out, doing something on his phone.

His eyebrows rose when he saw her. 'Are you going to be much longer?'

'I'm good to go.'

'Your hair's still wet.'

'It's a bit damp, that's all.' She'd towel-dried it as well as she could.

'It's cold outside.'

'My hairdryer's in Dublin.'

Pepe was fast beginning to recognise the look Cara threw at him as her 'if you'd let me get my stuff as I've asked you repeatedly, I wouldn't have this problem, ergo, this problem is *your* fault' look.

'I will ensure a hairdryer is here for you when we return from the vineyard.'

'I'm hoping my hair will be dry by then.'

'Hmm.' He gazed at her musingly. 'I would say sarcasm doesn't suit you but it actually does.'

She scowled. 'Funnily enough, it's only when I'm around you that my sarcastic gene comes out.'

'I will have to work hard to eradicate it,' he said, getting to his feet and leaning over to swipe her nose. She did have the cutest nose. 'And I'll work hard to eradicate the evil looks you keep throwing at me.'

'The only way that's going to happen is if you find *your* reasonable gene and let me return to Dublin.'

'You're welcome to return to Dublin any time you

like,' he said, smiling to disguise his irritation. 'I have made it clear what the consequences will be if you do so.'

'Like I said, you need to find your reasonable gene. Find it and I might lose my sarcastic gene.'

'I have already found my reasonable gene. It is unfortunate it differs from your definition of *reasonable* but there you go—you can't please everyone.' He expanded his hands and mocked a bow. 'Now, my fiery little geisha, it is time for us to leave.'

'What did you call me?' The look she gave him was no mere scowl. If looks could turn a man to stone he would now be made of granite.

'So touchy.'

'Calling me a geisha is pretty much on a par with calling me a concubine.'

'Not at all—a concubine is a permanent fixture in a man's life, there to give pleasure. A geisha is a hostess and an artiste. It is rare for a geisha to have sex with a male client.'

She didn't look in the slightest bit mollified. If anything, her scowl deepened.

'I can see I have my work cut out with you,' he said with a theatrical sigh. 'Maybe it is a good thing you will be with me for five months—I fear it will take me that long to get a smile out of you.'

Cara sat upright as they drove into a heliport, or whatever the name was for a field with a great big white helicopter with red Mastrangelo livery on it, and an enormous hangar right behind it.

Her stomach turned over at the sight of it. 'Please tell me we are not travelling in that thing?'

'It's either an eight-hour round trip to the vineyard by car, or we can do it in a quarter of the time in this beauty.'

'I vote for the car.'

'Sorry, *cucciola mia*, but I vote for the chopper. An hour there, an hour back.'

'It's a split vote.'

'It's my time and money.'

'Do I *have* to come? Can't I just wait here?'

'Yes, you do have to come.' For the first time she detected an edge to his voice. 'I'm not arguing with you again. I assure you, the ride will be perfectly safe and comfortable.' To prove his non-arguing point, he opened his door and got out.

She stuck her tongue out at his retreating form, watching as he joined a trio of men standing by the helicopter, all wearing black overalls. She guessed they were the flight crew.

The interior of the helicopter settled her nerves a touch. It was much less tinny than she had thought a helicopter would be. If anything, it was rather plush. She climbed aboard and sat down on a reclining white leather seat. Pepe showed her where all the big-boy-with-too-much-money gadgets were located on the seat, including a foldaway laptop.

'Aren't you sitting with me?' she asked, perturbed when he went to climb back out.

He grinned. 'One of us has to fly the thing.'

Before she could react, he'd jumped out and slid the door closed. In less than a minute he had opened the door at the front and made himself at home with the controls.

'Very funny, Mastrangelo,' she said, speaking over the low partition dividing them. If she wanted she could lean over and prod him. Which she was seriously considering doing if he didn't stop buggering about…

'Where's the pilot?' she asked, desperation suddenly lacing her voice.

He didn't look back, simply continued doing whatever he was doing with the range of knobs and buttons and thingies before him. 'Ladies and gentlemen, this is your captain speaking,' he said, amusement lacing his deep voice. 'For your own safety, Air Mastrangelo asks that you keep your seat belt fastened at all times and refrain from smoking for the duration of the flight.'

'You are having a laugh.'

He put some headphones on then turned his head back to look at her. 'Put your belt on, Cara—I promise you are in safe hands.'

'What about the men you were talking to? Aren't they going to fly it?'

'They were the maintenance crew.'

It was only when he turned the engine on that she truly believed Pepe was going to pilot it.

'Please,' she shouted over the noise of the propellers—who would have known it would be so *loud*?—'tell me you're only joking.'

'Belt on.' He started speaking into the mouthpiece of the headphone, talking in fluent French, his whole demeanour altering, adopting a serious hue.

'You can really fly this thing?' she asked when he'd stopped speaking and was doing stuff on the dashboard—was it even called a dashboard?

'I really can.'

'You're really qualified?'

'I really am. Have you got your seat belt on?'

'Yes.'

'Then we are good to go.'

And just like that, they were airborne.

And just like that, Cara's stomach lurched. She actually felt her half-eaten croissant and decaf coffee move inside her.

Slowly, the helicopter rose. At least it seemed slow, their ascent high above the heliport gradual.

Nothing was rushed. Everything in the cockpit was calm. And, as she watched him concentrate, watched him fly the beast they were in, her fears and nerves began to subside.

She'd ridden on planes many times, was used to the smoothness and almost hypnotic hum of the engines. This was different on so many levels.

There were so many things she wanted to ask him, not least of which was how did playboy extraordinaire Pepe Mastrangelo have the discipline to get his pilot's licence? His intelligence was not in doubt, but this was a man with the attention span of a goldfish—at least with women. She might know next to nothing about flying a helicopter but she knew for certain there was a lot more involved than learning to drive a car.

Surely it was something he would be proud to tell people? Never mind all the double dates they'd shared with Luca and Grace; they'd spent practically a whole weekend together, discussed all the vineyards he owned with his brother, discussed all the travelling he did between those vineyards as his brother liked to base himself on the family estate in Sicily, and not once had he mentioned flying his own helicopter. He hadn't even hinted at it.

As she looked at him now, relaxed but alert, clearly in his element...it was as if he'd been born to fly.

She wanted to bombard him with questions but, despite the unexpected smoothness of the flight—a smoothness she knew without having to be told came from the skill of his piloting—the nausea in her stomach was spreading, reaching the stage where all her concentration had to be devoted purely to breathing and swallowing the saliva that had filled her mouth.

'Everything okay in the back?' he called out to her.

'All dandy. Thank you.' She inhaled deeply and closed her eyes.

'There are sick bags in the side pocket of your chair,' he said after a few moments of silence had passed.

All she could manage was a grunt.

It was Cara's *thank you* that alerted Pepe to something being wrong. He'd guessed on the jet to Paris from Sicily that she was suffering from motion sickness, had kept a close eye on her sleeping form in case she awoke and needed attention, but nothing had come of it.

He'd piloted enough people in the past decade to know when someone was suffering from it. Right then, he could hear in the deepness of her breathing that she was one of the unfortunate ones. He didn't imagine she would extend politeness towards him under any other circumstance.

'There's a neck pillow in the side pocket too,' he called out over his shoulder, pressing the button to turn the air conditioning on. 'If you put it on it'll help keep your head stable. Find a fixed point in the horizon to focus on. I promise I will make the ride as smooth as I can. The conditions out there are good.'

He received another grunt in return.

If there was one thing he had learned it was that those afflicted by motion sickness were never in the mood for idle chit-chat. All he could do to help on any practical level was concentrate on the job in hand and do his best to keep the craft in as straight a motion as he could. He regretted not taking the 'doors off' approach, but at the time had thought it would probably terrify her if she was alone in the back.

Every now and then he would ask if she was okay and

get a grunt in return. He didn't hear any sound of retching or vomiting, so that was a plus.

By the time he landed on the field a few miles from the vineyard he was thinking of purchasing, all was silent.

When he climbed over the partition to help her out, he almost did a double take. He had never seen anyone turn that particular shade of green before. Except, maybe, the Incredible Hulk.

She'd taken his advice with the neck rest, but apart from that she'd clearly dealt with her malady in her own way, reclining her seat as far back as it would go and keeping her eyes scrunched closed. Her hands gripped an empty sick bag, her knuckles white.

He slid the door open to let the air in then went back to her. He crouched down and placed a hand lightly on her shoulder. 'We're here.'

Cara opened one eye and peered at him. Or was it a glare? He couldn't quite tell. 'I know. We've stopped moving.'

'Can you stand?'

'I'll try in a minute.' She snapped her eye shut again then sucked in a breath and swallowed loudly. 'By the way, if you try and carry me out of here, I will sock you one.'

'Just breathe.'

She filled her lungs.

'That's it. In through the nose and out through the mouth.'

'I do know how to breathe. I've been doing it all my life.' Her snappy retort was said with teeth that weren't so much gritted as sucked.

'That's a very clever trait to have,' he said gravely. He had to admit that, despite her green hue, there was something incredibly sexy about the way she sparred with him. 'I will give you five minutes for your body to right itself and if you're still not capable of walking I *will* carry you to the car.'

His threat did the trick as when he returned exactly five minutes later Cara was sitting upright with her eyes open.

She looked at him. 'I think I need your help getting to my feet.'

'You must be bad.' If he hadn't already seen with his eyes that she was unwell, her clammy skin would have definitely given the game away. Her hand gripped his wrist so tightly her neat but short nails dug into his flesh.

She leaned into him, allowing him to half drag her to the open door.

'It'll be easier for you to get out if you sit down—it's a bit of a gap at the best of times.' Not waiting for an argument, he helped her sit her shaky frame to the floor and dangle her legs out of the overhang.

Then he jumped down.

'Can you get down or do you need my help?' If it was anyone else he'd just pull them down the last few inches.

Her green eyes pierced into him. He could see how much it pained her to have to say, 'I need your help.'

He placed his hands on her waist. 'Put your arms around me.'

'Do I have to?'

'No. It'll probably be safer for you though.'

This time she gritted her teeth for real.

Tilting her head to the side and away from his gaze, she looped her arms around his neck, taking care not to touch him in anything but the loosest of fashions.

Deliberately, he closed the small gap between them, felt her heavy breasts crush against his chest. Not for the first time that day he felt a flicker of excitement stir inside him. It was nice to know he wasn't dead from the waist down as he'd been fearing in recent months.

As it was such a short distance for her feet to reach—although if she'd been a few inches taller she would probably have reached the ground from the sitting position—it was a simple matter of tugging her down onto terra firma.

She swayed into him, her cheek coming to rest against his chest, her arms dropping from his neck like deadened weights.

'I'm sorry,' she muttered.

'I'm not.' He slipped his arms around her waist to support her limp form, and enjoyed the feel of her soft curves pressing against the contrasting hardness of his body. She really was incredibly cuddly. She was also clearly unwell. 'Can you walk?'

'Yes.' There was a definite air of defiance in her affirmation, a defiance aimed at her own legs rather than him. 'Do *not* carry me.'

'Come. The car is waiting for us.'

Half dragging her, Pepe somehow managed to manoeuvre Cara the ten metres or so to the Land Rover.

Christophe Beauquet, the vineyard's current owner, was behind the wheel waiting for them. He made no effort to get out and welcome them and made only the briefest of grunts when Pepe helped Cara sit down in the front.

Pepe leaned over to strap her seat belt on, trying to ignore, again, her gorgeous scent. He could hear her furious swallowing, knew she was doing her best to keep back what her body was so desperate to expel. Her hand still clutched the sick bag.

'She needs to look forwards,' he explained before jumping into the back of the four-wheel drive.

Christophe didn't even try to hide his disgust. 'All this fuss for a short air ride?'

The hairs on Pepe's arms lifted. It took him a moment to realise it was his hackles rising. 'She's pregnant,' he answered shortly, leaning back into his seat and clamping his mouth into a firm line. He did not like the Frenchman's tone. He didn't like it *at all*.

CHAPTER SIX

WHEN CARA AWOKE it was dusky. Unlike when she'd awoken that morning, she didn't have the faintest idea where she was. The last thing she remembered was pulling up alongside a pretty farmhouse. Oh, and she remembered Pepe practically yanking her door open so she could vomit. How he knew she was waiting until the car stopped moving before giving in to it, she didn't have a clue. But he did know. And as she'd vomited out of the car and into the paper bag, he was by her side, rubbing her back and drawing her hair away from the danger zone.

It was support of a kind she'd never expected from him, and remembering it made her belly do a funny skip.

She patted her body, relieved to find herself fully dressed. She felt better. A little woozy, but on the whole much better.

When she sat up, she found her shoes, a gorgeous pair of flats from a designer brand she had coveted for years, laid neatly by the double bed she had been placed in.

She guessed she should get up and find Pepe. He was around somewhere, in this picture-book home.

It didn't take long to find him.

She shuffled out of the room and into an open landing. Below, she could hear voices. Walking carefully, she made her way down the stairs and followed the murmurs into a large kitchen.

Sitting around a sturdy oak table was Pepe, the man she remembered as Christophe and a tiny, birdlike woman. So small, the woman was inches shorter than Cara. It was like looking at Mrs Pepperpot come to life.

Mrs Pepperpot spotted her first and bustled over, taking Cara's arm and leading her over to join them, all the while gabbling away in French.

Pepe rose from his chair. 'Cara,' he said, pulling her into an embrace and kissing her on each cheek. 'How are you feeling?'

'Much better,' she mumbled.

'Good.' He stepped back and appraised her thoughtfully. A half-filled glass of wine lay before him. 'You are still a little too pale but you no longer look like the Incredible Hulk.'

'That's a bonus.' She sat on the chair he'd pulled out for her and budged it close to his. No sooner had she sat down when Mrs Pepperpot put a steaming bowl of what looked like a clear broth in front of her and a basket of baguettes.

'*Mangez,*' she ordered, putting her hands to her mouth in what looked like an imitation of eating.

'Cara, this is Christophe's wife, Simone,' Pepe said by way of introduction. 'She doesn't speak any English but she makes an excellent consommé.'

Cara gave Simone a quick smile. 'Thank you—*merci.*'

The consommé smelt delicious. Her starved belly rumbled. Loudly.

'*Mangez,*' Simone repeated.

'She's been waiting for you to wake up,' Pepe said. 'It's also thanks to her that the doctor made an impromptu home visit.'

Vaguely she remembered a heavily scented woman sitting on her bedside and prodding her with things. 'I thought I'd dreamt that.'

He laughed softly. 'You're four months pregnant. It seemed prudent to get you checked over in case you were suffering from something more serious than motion sickness.'

For all his jovial nonchalance, she knew she hadn't dreamt his concern. A strange warmth swept into her chest, suffusing her blood and skin with heat.

She turned her face away. 'I've suffered from motion sickness since I was a little girl. Pregnancy has just made it worse.'

'Even so, I've made arrangements for my family doctor to fly to Paris tomorrow to check you over. The doctor you saw here had concerns about your blood pressure being too low.'

'It's always been low,' she dismissed with a shrug.

'It is better to be safe. You have a child inside you that is dependent on your good health for its survival. I was going to get my doctor to check you over anyway, so I've just brought it forward by a few days.'

'Steady on, Pepe. You almost sound like a concerned father.'

His eyes flickered but the easy smile didn't leave his face.

Luckily any awkwardness was interrupted by Simone placing a jug of iced water in front of her and pouring Cara a glass.

'Why does she keep staring at me?' Cara muttered under her breath a few minutes later so only Pepe could hear. Simone kept nodding and beaming at her, unlike her surly husband, who did nothing but cradle his glass of wine. The Frenchwoman might not speak English but

Cara would bet Christophe knew more than enough to get by.

'Because you're pregnant and she wants to make sure you're getting the nutrition you need. You need to eat.'

'How can I eat when everyone's staring at me?'

For a moment she thought Pepe was going to make a wisecrack. Instead, he drew Christophe and Simone into conversation and, while the talk between them was of a serious tone, it worked, diverting their attention away from her.

Pepe was right about the consommé. It was delicious. Along with a still-warm bread roll, it filled her belly just enough.

It was at the moment she put her spoon in her empty dish that Christophe laughed at something Pepe said, downed his wine and held out a beefy hand. Pepe rose from his seat to take it and, leaning over the table, the two men shook hands vigorously, Christophe gripping Pepe's biceps.

'Is this a new form of male bonding?' Cara said in an aside to Pepe.

To her surprise, it was Christophe who answered. 'It is always good to formalise a deal with a shake of the hand.'

'You're buying the vineyard?' she asked Pepe.

'I would say it's more that Christophe has agreed to *sell* me the vineyard.' Pepe raised his glass in the Frenchman's direction. 'You drive a hard bargain, my friend.'

'Some bargains deserve to be hard fought.' Christophe lifted the wine bottle and made to refill Pepe's glass.

Pepe held out a hand to stop him. 'Not for me. I will be driving back to Paris shortly.'

'Driving?' Cara asked hopefully.

'*Sì.* I got some staff to bring a car over for us.'

'Where are they?'

'They've taken the helicopter back. Don't worry—I got the flight crew to come. They left about half an hour ago.'

For a moment she just stared at him, incredulous. 'Seriously? You got your pilots to drive all this way to drop off a car and then fly back?' How long had she been asleep? Five hours? He must have got the wheels in motion the second her head had hit the pillow.

He shrugged as if it were no big deal. 'They weren't doing anything else. It gave them a day out.'

'Did you do this…for *me*?'

'The helicopter's not long been reupholstered. I didn't want to risk you ruining it by upchucking everywhere.'

Somehow, she just knew Pepe could not give a flying monkey about upholstery.

'I thought we were going to a business dinner tonight?'

'I'm sure they can survive without our company for one night,' he said drily. 'I am not so cruel that I would force you to spend another hour in a craft that makes you violently ill for the sake of a dinner party with a handful of the most boring people in all of Paris.'

A compulsion, a strange, strange desire, tingled through her fingers to lace themselves through his.

Quickly she fisted her hands into balls.

So what if he'd displayed a hint at humanity?

It didn't mean she had to hold his hand.

It didn't change a thing.

By the time they left the vineyard, the sun had set and the Loire Valley was in darkness. The roads were clear, the drive smooth, but still Pepe was aware that Cara's breathing had deepened.

'Are you feeling all right?' he asked, turning the air conditioning up a notch.

'I think so.' Her head was back against the rest, her eyes shut.

'Open a window if it helps.' It was too dark to see the colour of her complexion, but he'd bet it had regained the green hue.

Cold air filtered through the small opening she made in the window, and she turned her face towards it, breathing the fresh air in.

'You say you've always suffered from motion sickness?' he said a few minutes later when he was reasonably certain she wasn't going to upchuck everywhere.

'As long as I can remember. Boats are the worst.'

'Have you been on many boats?'

'A couple of ferry crossings from England to Ireland when I was a teenager. I spent most of those hugging the toilet.'

'Sounds like fun.'

'It was—tremendous fun was had by all.'

He laughed softly. If there was one thing he liked about Cara it was her dry sense of humour.

He slowed the car a touch, keeping a keen eye out for any potholes or other potential hazards. The last thing he wanted was to do anything to increase her nausea.

'How long have you flown helicopters?' she asked.

'I got my licence about ten years ago.'

'I had no idea.'

'It's no big deal,' he dismissed.

'Sure it is. I assume it's more involved than passing a driving test?'

'Slightly,' he admitted, recalling the hundreds of flying hours he'd put in and the unrelenting exams. He'd loved every minute of it. And, he had to admit, his mother's pride when he'd received his pilot's licence had been something to cherish. Her pride was generally reserved for Luca.

'Are you going to make me fly in one again?'

'No.' He knew if he insisted, she would—ungraciously—comply. As he was fast learning, keeping Cara Delaney attached to him was proving trickier than first thought.

'So you're going to buy the vineyard, then?' she said, changing the subject.

'I am. It's a good, established business and the soil is of excellent quality.'

'How did you get Christophe to agree to sell it to you? He looked like he'd rather be wrestling bears than dealing with you when we arrived.'

'I think surliness is his default setting,' Pepe mused. 'He's one of those men who feel they have to prove their masculinity by puffing out their chest and pounding on it.'

He heard what sounded like a snigger. For a moment it was on the tip of his tongue to share how he'd been on the verge of telling the Frenchman that he could forget the sale, so incensed had he been by Christophe's attitude to Cara's nausea. If his wife, Simone, hadn't been such a welcome contrast, soothing Pepe's ruffled feathers and chiding her husband's surliness away, he would have refused to even take a tour.

Dealing with ultra-macho men was nothing new—he was Sicilian after all. Most men there drank testosterone for breakfast. Today, for the first time, he hadn't wanted to play the macho games such men demanded. He never gained any gratification from them. His own power was assured. There was no need to beat his chest or play a game of 'mine is bigger than yours'. Without being arrogant, he knew that went without saying—in *all* circumstances. But men like Christophe expected those games to be played. Today, for the first time, Pepe had refused.

He'd wanted to look after Cara.

His fingers tightened on the steering wheel as he recalled the way his stomach had clenched to see her so obviously unwell. Yes. A most peculiar feeling. Maladies did not normally bother him. People became ill, then, as a rule, people recovered. A fact of life.

Pregnancy was also a fact of life. As was motion sickness. Cara's suffering really shouldn't bother him beyond the usual realms of human decency.

Yet it did. It was taking all his self-restraint not to lay a comforting hand on her thigh. Saying that, if he were to lay a hand there, comforting or otherwise, she'd likely slap it.

'Are you going to run the deal by Luca first?' Her soft Irish lilt broke through his musings.

'No.' He spoke more sharply than he would have liked. 'No,' he repeated, moderating his tone. 'This is my domain. *I* run our dealings outside Sicily.'

'I thought Luca was in charge.'

'What made you think that? Is it because he's the older brother?'

'No. It's because he's the more steady and *reliable* brother.'

Even in the dark he knew his knuckles had whitened.

'Your brother might be as scary as the bogeyman but at least he conducts himself with something relatively close to decorum and thinks with more than his penis.'

Any minute and his knuckles would poke through his skin. 'Are you deliberately trying to pick an argument with me?'

'Yes.'

'Why?'

'Because I don't like it when you're nice to me.'

'Does driving you home constitute me being *nice*?'

'As opposed to you flying me back in that tin shack, then yes; yes, it does. And incidentally, you're not driving me *home*. You're driving me back to your house.'

'My home is your home until your baby is born.' Although, at that particular moment, he would take great pleasure in stopping the car, kicking her out and telling her to walk herself back to Paris.

Impossible, ungrateful woman.

Impossible *sexy* woman.

There was no denying it. Cara Delaney was as sexy as sin, and as much as he tried to keep his errant mind on the present, it insisted on going back sixteen weeks to what had been, in hindsight, the best weekend of his life.

'Would you prefer if I spent the next five or so months being horrible to you and having no consideration of your needs?'

'Yes.'

He cocked an eyebrow. 'Really?'

'The only niceness I want from you is my freedom.'

'You have your freedom. You are here under your own free will. You are welcome to leave at any time.'

'But for me to leave would mean a life of poverty for our child. Or at least, the start of its life would be full of poverty unless you do the decent thing and give me money to support him or her.'

'I will give you money to support our child when I have definitive proof that it *is* our child. I will not be played for a fool.'

He heard a sharp inhalation followed by a slow, steady exhalation.

'I really don't get it.'

'Get what?'

'Your cynicism.'

'I am not cynical.'

'You impregnated a virgin yet you refuse to believe your paternity without written proof. If that's not cynical, then I don't know what is. And I don't get why you are that way.'

'There is nothing to get. I do not take anything at face value. That's good business sense, not cynicism.' Much as he tried to hide it, a real edge had crept into his voice. He'd thought she would be grateful he was rearranging his schedule to drive her back to Paris, had assumed a little gratitude would soften her attitude towards him. But no. For all the softness of her curves and her bottom lip, Cara Delaney was as hard as nails.

From the periphery of his vision, he saw her straighten.

'Grace and I used to talk about you,' she said.

'Why doesn't that surprise me?'

'We used to wonder why you were the way you were.'

'I haven't the faintest idea what you're talking about.'

'You come from a loving family. You had two parents who loved and supported you and encouraged you...'

'That is what you used to say about me?' he interrupted with a burst of mocking laughter.

'Your mother dotes on you,' she said coldly. 'By all accounts your father doted on you too. You have a closer relationship with your brother than most siblings can dream of. *That's* what I mean about coming from a loving family.'

'*Sì,*' he conceded. 'My parents loved me. Luca and I are close. It is normal.'

'I have two stepsisters who hate me only fractionally less than they hate each other. I have a bunch of half-siblings scattered around Dublin whom I have never met. I have a mother who doesn't care a fig that I'm pregnant. I have a father who is unaware he's going to be a granddad, but that's because he's had no involvement in my life for over a decade.'

For a moment he didn't know what to say to that unexpected outburst or how to react to the raw emotion behind it. 'You haven't seen your father in ten years?'

'Thirteen years. My parents split when I was eleven. Mam and I moved to England when I was thirteen and I haven't seen him since.'

'My father died thirteen years ago.' Something in his chest moved as he thought of Cara going through her own personal trauma while his own life was shattering, first by the death of his father and then by Luisa's vile and ultimately devastating actions.

'I'm sorry.' Her voice softened. 'I've seen pictures of your dad—you look just like him.'

'*Sì*. He was a very handsome man.'

This time she did laugh. 'Oh, you are so full of yourself.'

'You can be full of me too if you want.'

'Are you trying to make me sick again?'

He chuckled, glancing over at her, certain there was the trace of a smile playing on her lips.

Mind out of the gutter, he chided himself. He needed to keep his attention focused on the road before him, not on memories of burying himself inside her tight sweetness.

All the same, he took a sharp breath in the hope it would loosen the tightness in his groin.

'Did your mother stop your father from seeing you after she left him?'

'No. He stopped himself from seeing me. It was too much hassle for him to go across the Irish channel and see his eldest child. We exchange Christmas cards and that's it.'

For a moment he thought she was going to say something else, but when he glanced at her, he saw her eyes were closed and she was massaging her forehead. For all her bitterness there was a definite vulnerability about her when she spoke of her parents.

'Did you miss him?'

'My father?'

'Yes. It must have been a hard time for you.'

She laughed, a noise that sounded as if it were being done through a sucked lemon. 'If anything, it was a relief. My father is a serial shagger. He cheated on my mum so many times I think even *he* lost count.'

'Were you aware of this at the time?' Surely her father would have been discreet?

'I've always known, even when I was too young to understand. They never bothered keeping it a secret from me. I caught him out twice—once when I was going to the park with my friends and walked past the local pub and saw him through the window draped over some woman.'

'He was with another woman in your local pub?' Even Pepe, who was not easily shocked, was shocked at this.

'You think that's bad?' Her tone rose in pitch. 'The next time I caught him out, which couldn't have been more than six months later, I found him in the marital bed with another woman—a different woman from the woman he was with in the pub.'

'You caught him in the act?'

'No, thank God. They were lying in bed. I remember my dad was smoking a cigarette. I don't know what shocked me the most—I'd no idea he was a smoker.'

And Cara had no idea why she was sharing all this with Pepe of all people.

It had been the same over the weekend they'd shared together. He was such an easy person to talk to and had such an unerring ability to make the person he was with—namely her—believe that every word she uttered was worth listening to, that it was quite possible to spill your guts to him without even realising. He'd done it then, listened to her rabbit on for hours about her love of her job, her hopes for the future.

No one had ever made her feel like that before.

He'd made her believe she was special.

It would be all too easy to believe it again.

She opened the window a little further and practically stuck her nose out of it, inhaling the cold air gratefully. It compressed the anger and pain of those horrible memories back down to a manageable level.

Silence sprang between them, a silence that was on the verge of becoming uncomfortable when Pepe said, 'What did you do? Did you tell your mother?'

She sucked in more cold air before answering. 'Yes. Yes, I did. He didn't even bother to deny it. She threw him out for all of two days before taking him back. She always took him back.'

Her stomach twisted a little more as she recalled hearing them 'make up'. They hadn't cared that their ten-year-old daughter was in the house. They'd never cared.

Her entire childhood had revolved around her father's affairs and her mother's reactions to them. Those reactions had never been about Cara. Their daughter had been secondary to everything in their sick marriage where sex was a weapon used to hurt each other in the most cruel and demeaning ways.

'I always swore I'd never get involved with a man who was like my father, so more fool me.'

'What do you mean by that?'

'You,' she practically spat. 'How else do you think

my dad was able to pull so many women and use them so badly? He's a charmer, just like you are.'

'I am *nothing* like your father.' His vehemence was the most emphatic she had ever heard him.

'You use women for your own gratification with no thoughts of them as real people.'

'That is utter rubbish. I have never cheated on anyone. Ever.' An ugly tone curdled his words. 'I despise cheats.'

'You still use women.'

'I do not use women. I am never anything but honest with my lovers. Do not kid yourself into believing they are in my bed under false pretences.'

'You used me. I thought you wanted me in your bed because you wanted *me*. I had no idea you wanted to get your hands on my stupid phone and not my body.'

It was Pepe's turn to suck in a breath. 'I accept that I used you, Cara. I am not proud of what I did but it had to be done. My brother was a man on the verge of a breakdown. It doesn't change the fact that I found you as sexy as hell. I still do. I wanted to make love to you regardless of the circumstances.'

'You still used me. You can tell me until you're blue in the face that you're nothing like my father but I know better. You're two of a kind. You make love to women and then dump them, leaving them to deal with the emotional fallout. And the unwanted after-effects. Like babies,' she couldn't resist adding.

A screech of brakes and a swerve of the wheels as he brought the Mercedes to a shuddering halt on the verge.

Pepe turned the engine off, his breathing ragged.

Cara took little consolation that she had finally pierced his charming armour.

For long moments the only sound was their breathing.

'I am going to start driving again in a moment,' he

said grimly. 'Unless you want me to leave you to make your own way back to Paris, I suggest you do not speak to me, other than to say if you're feeling ill.'

From the tone of his voice, she knew he meant every word.

CHAPTER SEVEN

IT WAS NO USE. Sleep really had no intention of coming. She could count as many sheep as she liked but they might as well be blowing big fat raspberries at her for all the use they were at getting her off to slumber.

Cara climbed out of bed and reached for her new robe, which was more of a kimono. However much she might tell herself that she was itching to get her well-worn flannelette dressing gown back, there was no getting around the fact this scarlet silk kimono was utterly gorgeous and felt like liquid on her skin.

After three days in Pepe's Parisian home she still wasn't as familiar with the layout as she should be, but she knew her way to the kitchen.

She hadn't seen much of him since their drive back from the Loire Valley. Instead of keeping her chained to him, he'd had a change of heart and now insisted she be chained to Monique the housekeeper instead. Okay, maybe that was a slight exaggeration. What he had actually said, when they'd arrived back at the house after almost three hours of ice between them, was that all his meetings for the rest of the week were in Paris and that she was free to stay at home if she would prefer. Just as she'd thought he was becoming a more reasonable human being, he'd qualified it with, 'Monique is around during the day. She can accompany you if you need to go anywhere.'

'Where is there for me to go?' she'd shot back. 'I don't speak the language and I don't have any money to do anything. Parisian prices are stupidly high.'

He'd shrugged without looking at her. 'I have a swimming pool and spa—you're welcome to use them whenever you wish. Besides, if the paternity test proves your child is mine then you'll have more money than you know how to spend.'

She'd responded by calling him a name that would have made the nuns from the convent she'd attended before moving to England blush.

The following morning he'd made matters even worse by having a top-of-the-range laptop, smartphone and e-reader delivered to the house for her. The e-reader had, from what she'd been able to ascertain, unlimited credit installed. She'd taken a perverse pleasure in downloading as many books as she could, all featuring the most unheroic, misogynistic protagonists that she could find. Hopefully Pepe would receive an itemised bill with all the titles listed for him.

She hated that he would do something thoughtful. It was the same as when he'd driven her home rather than make her fly back in the helicopter. She didn't want him to be *nice*. She wasn't going to be like her mother and forgive deplorable behaviour because of a stupid gift.

Making her way down the winding staircase, she headed for the kitchen. The house was in darkness but for the dim glow of night lights that were strategically placed throughout.

She switched on the main light of the kitchen, blinking several times as her eyes adjusted to the brightness.

It felt strange being in there, in a kitchen as large as

the house she'd grown up in, feeling as if she were an intruder. She had no idea where anything was but found the fridge easily enough—seeing as it was a whopping American-style fridge large enough to use in a mortuary, it would have been hard to miss.

What she really wanted was some warm milk. Grace's mother, Billie, would make it for them when she went for one of her frequent sleepovers there. It was comforting. Now, if only she knew where to even begin searching for a saucepan...

The whisper of movement froze her to the spot. Her hand gripped the plastic milk carton.

'You're up late, *cucciola mia*,' a deep Sicilian drawl said from behind her.

She spun around to find Pepe striding languorously towards her. 'You scared the life out of me,' she snapped. Or, at least she tried to snap, but her mini-fright had left her a little breathless. Seeing all six feet plus of semi-naked Pepe also did something to her pulse-rate, but there he was, muscle-bound and gorgeous, and wearing nothing but a pair of low-slung jeans that perfectly accentuated his snake hips and showed his taut, olive chest to perfection. The silky hair that ran from his chest and down in a thin line over his toned stomach, thickened where the buttons of his jeans were undone...

His hair was tousled, black stubble breaking out along his jawline, almost as thick as his trimmed goatee.

Sin. That was what he looked like. A walking, talking advertisement for sin. And temptation.

'I didn't mean to scare you,' he said, not looking the least apologetic. 'I heard noise and came to investigate.'

'I couldn't sleep.'

His deep blue eyes held hers, meaning swirling in them. 'Nor could I.'

She broke the lock first, aware of warmth suffusing more than just her face.

'What brings you out of hiding?' he asked, standing a little closer than she would have liked.

She took a step back. 'I've not been in hiding.'

'You've barely left your room in three days. Monique says you've been no further than the dining room.'

'This isn't my home. I don't feel comfortable roaming around as if I belong here.' She felt especially uncomfortable now, but in an entirely different way, in a 'sexy half-naked man in front of me' kind of way.

She must be delirious. Sleep deprivation could do that.

'You *do* belong here. While you are under my roof, this is your home. You are free to treat it as you wish.'

'Except leave it.'

'You are always free to leave.'

She bit back the comment that wanted to break free. What was the point? It would only be a rehash of all their other arguments regarding her freedom.

'I was after some warm milk,' she muttered. 'I thought it would help me sleep.'

'I thought I heard you thrashing about in your bed.' At her quizzical expression, he added, 'My room is next to yours.'

'Oh.'

'You didn't know?' His lips quirked into a smirk.

'No. I didn't.' It shouldn't matter where Pepe slept. He could sleep in a shed for all she cared. But the room next to hers…?

Why the thought should heat her veins, she had no idea.

The playful, sensuous expression in his eyes softened a touch. 'I make a mean hot chocolate.'

It took a moment for her to realise he was offering to make her some. 'Thank you.'

He started busying himself, opening doors and rifling through drawers.

She suppressed a snigger and hoicked herself up on the kitchen table. 'You don't know your way around your kitchen any better than I do.'

'Guilty as charged.' He knelt down and leaned into a cupboard, giving her an excellent view of his tight buttocks straining against the denim. 'I employ housekeepers so I don't have to know my way around my kitchens. When I'm home alone, take-out is my best friend.'

Oh, the blasé way he pluralised *kitchen*! Cara thought of the poky galley kitchen she shared—*had* shared—with three other women. It would probably fit in Pepe's fridge.

When he reappeared he had a milk pan in his hand. 'It would be quicker to microwave it but my mother always taught me it was sacrilege to make a hot chocolate like that.'

'I thought you had a fleet of staff when you were growing up?'

'We did,' he said, matter-of-factly. 'But making our nightly hot chocolate was a job my mother always liked to do herself. She used to sit Luca and I on the kitchen table—much as you're sitting now—while she made it.'

'It sounds wonderful,' she said with more than a touch of envy. Evenings in the Delaney household had normally consisted of her mother fretting about where her father was.

He cocked his head while he thought about it. A glimmer of surprise flittered across his features. 'Yes, it was.'

Pepe added the expensive cocoa powder to the warming milk before spooning some sugar into the mixture, whisking vigorously as he went along.

Looking at his childhood from Cara's perspective, he could see it had been idyllic. His feelings about being spare to Luca's heir were not something that had developed until he'd hit his teenage years, but Luca had always been the good one, whereas he'd always been the naughty one. Looking back, it was as if his parents' expectations of him had been lower from the start.

Or had it been that their expectations of Luca had been set too high? His brother had been groomed to take over the family business. He'd had responsibility thrust upon him from the womb. For Pepe, the only responsibility he'd had—and it was a self-imposed one—was to make his serious big brother laugh.

He whipped the milk pan away from the heat right before it reached boiling point, then poured it into the two waiting mugs.

When he turned to pass Cara her drink, his chest compressed.

Her short legs dangled from the table, hovering inches above the floor, and she was chewing on her bottom lip.

He wondered if she knew the top of her robe had parted a touch, giving him a tantalising glimpse of that wonderful cleavage his senses remembered so well. The first time he'd buried himself in those glorious breasts he'd thought he'd died and gone to heaven.

During the intervening months the wonder of that night was something he had suppressed with a ruthlessness he'd never before had to employ. But it had always been there, hovering in the periphery of his memories, taunting him, tantalising him. Often it would catch him unawares, a visual memory or a familiar scent, always with the same end result, a burst of need that would shoot straight to his groin and clutch at his chest. The same burst of need he was currently experiencing. The same need that had been a semi-permanent ache since he'd stood next to Cara at the font at Lily's christening.

Under normal circumstances, that one night wouldn't have been the end of them. He would have gone back for more. Hell, he might even have brought her here to Paris as he'd insinuated, but not for the sake of his art collection. No, he'd have brought her here so he could devour that delectable body over and over until he was finally spent and there was nothing left for him to discover and enjoy.

As she reached out a hand to take the mug, her kimono strained against her breasts, moulding them for his hungry eyes, and the need in his groin tightened, straining against the denim he wore.

The hem of the kimono barely covered her knees.

Was she wearing *anything* beneath it?

'What are you doing?' Cara's voice was a husky whisper.

Without even realising it, he'd closed the gap between them. One more step and he'd be able to part her creamy thighs and slip between them…

Cara's heart thumped so strongly she could hear it pound against her ribs.

'I asked, what are you doing?' How she managed to drag the words out, she didn't know. Pepe was so close he'd sucked all the air from her lungs.

His large warm hand closed over hers and removed the mug, placing it on the table, out of her reach.

And then he was cupping her cheeks, forcing her to meet his stare. 'I'm going to kiss you.'

'No!' It was more of a whimper than a refusal. She tried to wrench her face free from his clasp but his hold was too strong. And, somehow, too gentle.

'*Sì.*' He brushed a thumb over her bottom lip. 'Yes, *cucciola mia.* I am going to kiss you.'

She didn't want to respond. God alone knew she didn't want to respond.

Yet when his lips slanted onto hers and held there for long moments before prising her mouth apart, and when his thick tongue slipped into her mouth, the only word revolving around and around in her head was *yes*. Yes. Yes. Yes.

The only answer her body gave was yes.

The hands she tried to ball into fists fought back, tracing up his bare biceps and clinging to his shoulders, her nails digging into the smooth flesh.

And still she tried to fight. Desperately she fought against the growing rip tide of need pulsating through her blood, fought against the moisture bubbling in her most intimate area.

But mostly she battled for her head, a fight she was so far from winning she…

His hand was cupping her breast.

When had that happened…?

It felt so…good. Wonderful. His touch…

But it wasn't enough. The silk of the kimono was too restrictive.

Pepe must have read her mind because he slipped a hand beneath the thin material and spread it whole against a breast so sensitive, the relief of him finally touching it—touching her—made her gasp into his hot mouth.

And then she was kissing him back, her lips moving against his with no conscious thought, her tongue dancing against his, her whole body alive to his touch, the heat from his mouth and the taste of *him*.

Roughly he tugged her kimono apart, exposing her

naked flesh. He snaked an arm around her waist and pulled her flush to him, crushing her breasts against his chest, crushing her mouth with an ever deepening kiss, his other hand trailing up her back, up the nape of her neck and then spearing her hair, gently tugging at it, before trailing back and reaching down to take her hand, which he placed on the front of his jeans. His fingers curled into hers as he pressed her hand tight to him. Even through the thick denim she could feel the length and weight of his erection. She could feel the heat emanating from him.

It was a heat her starved body revelled in.

Because it had been starving.

It had been starving for *him*.

He had brought her to life, given her an appetite she hadn't known she had, and then he'd left her. Alone. And pregnant.

'See, *cucciola mia*,' he said, breaking his mouth away and dragging kisses across her cheek and down her neck. 'This is how badly I want you. Enough that I think I might explode if I don't have you.'

His words, the sound of his voice, were things the small part of her shrieking at her treacherous body anchored onto, using them to bring her out of this erotic stupor he had put her in.

Somehow she managed to wedge her hands between their meshed chests—and, God, her body really didn't want her to; her lips ached for just one more kiss, the apex of her thighs begged her to let him continue—and, using all the strength she could muster, pushed him away.

'I said *no*.'

He almost reeled back.

Pepe's chest heaved as he stared at her with eyes that penetrated, almost as if he were reaching into the deepest recess of her mind. 'Your mouth said no. The rest of you said yes.'

Although his words were nothing but the truth, she shook her head, her shaking hands frantically wrapping the kimono back up, tying it as tightly as was physically possible. 'When a woman says no, then the answer is no. No, no, no. You have no right to help yourself to me.'

His face contorted and he took another step back. 'Do *not* imply that I am some sort of rapist. You wanted me as much as I wanted you. You kissed me back. You enjoyed every minute of it.'

The savagery of his words made her flinch.

To compound it all, she felt hot tears sting the backs of her retinas. 'I don't care how much I *enjoyed* it,' she said, forcing the words out, aware her words were hitched. 'This is not going to happen. Unlike you, my brain is in control of my actions.'

His lips curved into something that was supposed to resemble a smile. 'You think? Well, *cucciola mia*, you will learn that my control is second to none. Have no worries—I will not touch you again. Not without a written contract from you saying yes.'

With that parting shot, he strolled out of the kitchen, leaving her rooted to the table she was still sitting upon.

CHAPTER EIGHT

PEPE GROWLED AT the screen before him. The words of the contract could be in gobbledegook for all he cared.

There was no point lying to himself. He was angry. Angry at Cara. Angry at the situation they had been forced into. Angry at himself.

But especially angry at her.

He'd never forced himself on a woman in his life. Never. He despised men who did such things, thought castration too mild a punishment for such deeds.

Had he really misread the situation so badly?

No. Absolutely not.

Cara had the most expressive face of any woman he'd ever known. They said that eyes were windows to the soul. With Cara, her eyes were windows to her emotions. If she was angry, happy, tired or ill, her eyes were the signposts for him to follow.

How had he become an expert on her *emotions*?

He shook his head briskly and rubbed his eyes. He probably wouldn't feel so crummy if he'd managed to get any sleep. But how was a man supposed to sleep when his body ached with unfulfilled desire?

One thing he was not, though, was hurt. His ego might be a touch bruised but, on a personal level, it made no difference if Cara was willing to share a bed with him or not. There were plenty of women out there who were. And in reality, it was probably better that they didn't resume a sexual relationship, especially as she was of a completely different mindset from his usual lovers.

He doubted there would ever come a time he would be able to bump into Cara at a party, sidle over to her, maybe give her bottom a cheeky pinch, and then catch up on old times.

The animosity would always be there.

In any case, if her baby did prove to be his, then he had to concede she would be a huge part of his life...well, for the rest of his life. If the baby was his then they would be for ever united, even in the most cerebral fashion.

An image of a tiny baby with a shock of Cara's flamered hair came into his head, an image he blinked away along with the nagging voice that kept piping up, asking him if he really wanted nothing more than to be a part-time father.

He clenched his hands into fists.

He didn't want to think that far ahead.

He didn't want to imagine how he would feel if Cara really was carrying his child.

Once, a long time ago, he'd been caught up in the magic of pregnancy, the unmitigated joy and wonder of knowing he had shared in the creation of life and that soon he would be a father. The child had been no more than a foetus but already he had loved it, had thought of the future that child would have with him and Luisa, and the family they would create together.

His child would never have felt second best.

His child never got the chance to feel anything, least of all second best.

Luisa had ripped that chance away from him.

Cara was nothing like Luisa.

Cara was like no one he'd ever met.

But what did he know of her *really*? He'd known Luisa pretty much all of his life but he'd never guessed she was capable of ripping his heart out and stamping on the remnants.

He would never trust another woman. He couldn't. There was only so much pain one man could take and he'd reached that limit before he'd even finished his teenage years.

Only when Cara's baby was born and the paternity test established that he truly was the father would he allow himself to think properly of the future.

Only then would he allow himself to think of what it truly meant to have a child.

Until that time came, his life would continue as it was. Except with a houseguest. A fiery, sexy houseguest.

Suppressing a yawn, he checked his watch. It was time to call it a day. There was a party he had to attend, a party he'd been looking forward to until approximately five days ago, being hosted by a good friend who was celebrating his first wedding anniversary. Not feeling in the mood to drive, he got his driver to take him home, all the while trying to shake himself out of the melancholic mood that had crept under his skin.

By the time he arrived back at his home he felt no better, but, with practised ease, slipped his old faithful smile on and strolled into the house.

'Where is Cara?' he asked Monique, who had hurried out to greet him.

'In her room.'

'Has she left it today?'

'Only for her lunch and a late afternoon snack.'

'Did she eat any breakfast?'

'A croissant and an apple.'

He headed to his room, refusing to reflect on his need to monitor Cara's eating habits. It was simple concern extended towards a pregnant woman, nothing more.

As he passed, Cara's bedroom door opened. Her eyes widened to see him and she took a step back, would no doubt have shut the door in his face if he hadn't stuck a foot in the doorway to prevent her.

'Good evening, *cucciola mia*. How has your day been?'

'Long and boring.'

'Then it must be a source of comfort to know we are going out tonight.'

She pulled a face but opened the door properly and leaned against the door frame, hugging her arms around her chest. 'It's getting late. Do I have to go?'

'Yes.'

'Can't I stay here with Monique?'

'Monique goes home at weekends—aren't you lucky? You can have me all to yourself.'

Her cheeks coloured and she scowled. 'How thrilling. Can't you get another babysitter for me?'

'It's too short notice. Besides, I don't think I could afford to pay anyone else to put up with you.'

'I'm no bother. I just stay in my room. It's like babysitting a five-year-old.'

Anyone listening in on them would be amused at the dryness of their conversation. If they were to scratch a little under the surface it would be a whole different story. The second her door had opened, Pepe's heart had begun to thunder, the weight in his gut twisting and clenching. The half-smile on his face could have been drawn on.

As for Cara…her beautiful lips were pulled in and tight, while her green eyes spat fire at him.

He wanted to touch her. He wanted to pick her up and

carry her across the room, lay her on the bed and make love to every inch of her.

After the way she had reacted in the kitchen in the early hours, it would be a long day in hell before he touched her again. She would have to get down on her knees and beg before he would even consider making love to her.

All the same, he couldn't resist reaching out a hand and tapping her cute little nose. 'We leave in an hour, *cucciola mia*. Cocktail dress. Be ready or I'll come in your room and help you.'

'You wouldn't dare.'

'Is that a challenge?'

'No!'

'In that case, be ready on time. I need to shower—see you in sixty minutes.'

Exactly one hour later, Pepe knocked on Cara's bedroom door. He half hoped she *wasn't* ready.

Forget the good talking-to he'd given himself earlier about not resuming their sexual relationship; just three minutes sparring outside her bedroom had laid waste to those good intentions.

There was something so damn sexy about his red-headed geisha.

If only she really were a geisha. Or better still, his own personal concubine. He was pretty sure bitching at her master wasn't part of either's job description. Geisha or concubine, all the woman concerned herself with was her master's pleasure. Seeing as it was pleasure of a sexual nature he wanted from Cara, he would much rather settle with concubine.

He was certain she did it deliberately, but she made him wait a full sixty seconds before opening her door.

The wait was worth it.

The quip he had ready on his lips blew away as his mouth fell open.

Pepe was used to dating beauties. He shamelessly used his wealth, charm and looks to pick the cream of the crop. Yet Cara outshone all of them.

Dressed in a richly red silk floor-length dress that showed off her curves, the sleeves skimming her shoulders to leave her arms bare, her glorious hair piled into a sleek chignon, she looked stunning. In her ears were heart drop crystals that shimmered under the light, and on her feet were shoes that had the same shimmering effect. Her make-up was subtle bar the lipstick, a rich red that perfectly matched her dress and made her kissable lips infinitely more so.

'Mio Dio,' he said appreciatively. 'You are beautiful.'

'It's amazing what money can do,' she said tartly, although her cheeks flamed to match her hair, her dress, her lips…

'You are Hestia come to life,' he breathed.

'That's appropriate seeing as the Vestal Virgins get their name from her Roman counterpart.'

A smile escaped his lips. 'She was also the Roman Goddess of the Hearth—of fire.'

'And I bet you see yourself as Eros—wouldn't you just love to get your hands on the Vestals?'

His smile tightened. 'Actually, no. I've found virgins too needy for my taste.'

It was a low blow and one he wished he could take back as soon as it escaped his lips. There was something about her spiky tongue that he reacted to. Her barbs penetrated him like no one else's.

Cara's eyes narrowed but she raised her chin and pulled the door shut behind her, her movements releasing a cloud of her perfume. 'Then we are better suited than I believed. I've always found lustful men too immature for *my* tastes.'

'How are you going to introduce me to your friends?' Cara asked as they sat in the back of the blacked-out Mercedes through the dark Parisian evening. The city twinkled with what seemed a million lights, giving it a magical quality that enthralled her.

'As my companion.'

'Is that how you introduce all your lovers?'

'I wasn't aware that you were my lover,' he responded easily, the coolness he'd displayed since she'd made the jibe about him being immature having dispersed. She much preferred it when he was cool towards her. It made it much easier to hate him.

'I suppose you can always introduce me as your pregnant one-night stand who you're waiting to give birth so you can get a paternity test to prove that you're the daddy.'

She felt him tense, knew that beneath his tuxedo his frame had tautened.

'Why are you happy to dress in a suit for business and wear a DJ for a party, but refuse to make an effort for your own niece's christening?' she asked, blurting out one of the many questions that played on her mind.

'I wasn't aware I hadn't made an effort for it,' he answered coolly.

She shrugged. Pepe's choice of attire was none of her business. 'So where is this party?'

'In Montmartre.'

Now he mentioned it, the lights of the sprawling hill that comprised Montmartre gleamed before them, the white Basilica of Sacre-Coeur sitting atop, almost surveying all beneath it. As they drove into the bustling arrondissement, she pressed her face to the window to take in the beautiful architecture, ambling tourists and nonchalant locals.

'How are you feeling?' he asked. 'Any nausea?'

'So far so good,' she confirmed.

'That is good.' Not trusting the casual tone to his voice, she looked at him and found him holding a paper bag aloft. He winked. 'Just in case.'

Despite herself, she laughed, the action loosening a little of the angst in her chest.

He moved closer to her and pointed out of the window. 'Through those gardens is the Musée de Montmartre. It is reputed to be the oldest house in Montmartre.'

'Didn't Renoir live in it?' she asked, wholly aware of his thigh now pressed against hers.

'Not quite—there is a mansion behind it that he lived in for a while. Maurice Utrillo lived there though.'

As they snaked their way through the cobbled streets, he pointed out more features of interest, his words breathing life into the ancient buildings, especially from the Impressionist era. He knew so much about the district, had such lively knowledge, his heavy Sicilian accent so lyrical it was a joy to listen to him.

Cara hid her disappointment when the driver came to a stop in a narrow street lined by a terrace of whitewashed five-storey homes, cafés and shops. She could have happily continued with their tour.

To her surprise, they went into a packed poky café that smelt strongly of coffee, body odour and illicit cigarettes. Pepe greeted the staff personally with his usual enthusiasm, shaking hands and kissing cheeks, before leading her through the back and out into a small courtyard.

'Ladies first,' he said, waving his hand at a flimsy-looking iron staircase that led all the way to the top floor. 'Don't worry,' he added, clearly reading her mind. 'I assure you it is safe.'

'Aren't there indoor stairs?' She was in no way mollified by his assurance.

'There are, but as you have seen, the café is busy, and if all tonight's guests were to use them, we would get in the way of the staff.'

'So why go through the front entrance? Why not get your driver to drop us off at the back?'

'Because the staff would be most put out if they knew I had been here and hadn't dropped in to say hello.'

'You do have a high opinion of yourself,' she muttered.

His smile dropped a wattage before the teeth flashed. 'Forgive my modesty but I am a good employer.'

Her brow knotted.

'I own the building,' he clarified.

'I thought you owned vineyards.'

'I do. Didn't you know variety is the spice of life?'

She sniffed pointedly, and hugged her wrap closer around her chest, wishing she had worn the thick designer coat Pepe had bought her. 'I'm surprised you haven't turned it into a high-tech hotel.'

He pulled a face. 'And rip it of its charm? This street is old-style Montmartre, unaffected and barely known by the tourists that have infected much of the rest of this glorious place. I intend to keep it that way.'

'You own the entire street?'

He inclined his head in affirmation then looked back to the iron stairs. 'Shall we?'

'I don't know…'

'Do you suffer from vertigo?'

'No.'

'Then where's your sense of adventure?'

'I've never had one.'

'Liar. You spent a year travelling Europe with Grace, so don't tell me you have no sense of adventure.'

'I'm pregnant.'

'Are pregnant women not able to climb stairs?'

'Don't be silly.'

His features softened. 'Cara, I promise I would never allow anything to happen to you or your baby. This staircase is only a couple of years old—I oversaw its construction myself. I'll be right behind you—I promise you'll be safe.'

Much as she knew she must be a fool to believe him, she found herself putting a foot onto the bottom step, half expecting the whole thing to come crashing down on them.

It was a lot sturdier than she anticipated. And, she had to admit, knowing he would be there to catch her if she should trip was…comforting. Pepe's strength and assurance were more than a little comforting.

'Which floor are we going to?' she asked, turning her head to look at him.

The grin that spread across his face made her stomach flip over. 'You and I, *cucciola mia*, are going all the way.'

Her cheeks burning at the suggestion in his tone, she climbed up, slowly at first until she became aware that Pepe, being a couple of paces behind her, had an excellent view of her derrière. Yep, knowing he had a face full of her backside certainly acted as rocket fuel and she reached the top in no time.

She had no idea what she'd been expecting: from the general dilapidation of the café below, she'd half assumed Pepe had made her dress up as a joke, but she certainly hadn't been expecting *this*.

The party was being held in a loft conversion. Except it was nothing like any loft she'd ever been in. Extremely large and airy, simply decorated with what she would refer to as faux shabby chic, it must have covered the length of the entire terrace.

'So do you own this loft too?'

He raised a brow.

'I know; a silly question. But this place…' Her voice trailed off.

'A little different from the café on the ground floor?'

'Yes. Exactly.'

'The café is a fixture in Montmartre. I didn't want to make any changes other than have it fitted with a kitchen that wasn't liable to catch fire at any moment. This loft, on the other hand, was begging to be converted into a proper work and living space.'

'Is it a studio?' There might be so many people crammed into the space that she couldn't see any art paraphernalia, but she'd recognise the smell of turps anywhere—with an artist for best friend, that was a given.

'*Sì.*' He nodded at a diminutive man holding court to a large crowd of glamorous people. 'That is the tenant, Georges Ramirez.'

'I know him,' she said, awed. 'Well, I know *of* him. We've auctioned his work before.'

'He's an old friend. The loft was designed with him in mind.'

As he spoke, Georges looked in their direction and spotted Pepe. His little gang looked too and in the click of a finger two dozen pairs of eyes had widened and two dozen sets of lips had curled into smiles. A few people, including Georges and the pretty woman clutching his hand, broke from the crowd and headed towards them.

In a whirl of French and English, and some Italian and

Spanish, Pepe presented her to people who were clearly his friends, introducing her simply as Cara with no further explanation. Names were thrown at her, hands shaken and embraces exchanged—well, embraces with Pepe were exchanged. All the while she stood there wishing the floor would open up and swallow her, whisk her away to somewhere familiar and calming.

Her hands had gone clammy, her pulse racing. 'I need to use the bathroom,' she whispered for Pepe's ears only, trying to keep any trace of panic from her voice.

He stared at her with a quizzical expression before inclining his head. 'The bathroom is through that door on the left of the bar,' he said, pointing at a long table pushed against a far wall, piled high with all manner of alcohol and soft drinks. 'Go through it and then it's the second door on the right.'

The door by the bar led into another enormous, brightly lit space. Canvases and sculptures were crammed inside, protected by a large stand-up sign that read 'Any Person Found Touching The Work Will Be Chemically Castrated'. An unexpected giggle escaped from her mouth.

Luckily the bathroom was empty and gave her time to collect herself.

She hated crowds. Hated large parties. Especially hated crowds and large parties where she didn't know anyone. It was that *new girl* feeling all over again, the knowledge that everyone was already acquainted with their own little friendship bands. Outsiders were most definitely *not* welcome. Outsiders on the arm of the man who was definitely the alpha male of the pack were as welcome as anthrax.

When she finally left her sanctuary, a tall brunette with the most amazing hazel eyes blocked her way. 'Ah, so *you're* my replacement,' she said with a dazzling smile.

CHAPTER NINE

'SORRY?' CARA DIDN'T have the faintest idea what she was talking about.

'I was Pepe's original date for the evening,' the beauty said without the slightest trace of rancour.

Cara didn't know what to say, could feel herself shrinking from the inside out.

'It is not a problem,' the beauty assured her. 'We used to date but it was over a long time ago. I'm sure we'll hook up again some other time when he's back on the market and in need of a semi-platonic date for the evening. In the meantime, you should enjoy him while you have him.'

Cara searched for signs the woman was having a joke at her expense but saw nothing but open friendliness in those hazel eyes. She swallowed and forced her rooted tongue to work. 'What does *semi-platonic* mean?'

'Oh, you know—what is the English expression?' Her eyes scrunched up as she thought, then another beaming smile broke out on her spectacularly pretty face. 'I know—it means "friends with benefits"!'

'Friends with benefits,' Cara echoed weakly, her stomach roiling at the thought.

That friendliness turned to consternation. 'Have I spoken out of turn?'

'Not at all,' Cara said, knowing as she said the words that they sounded weedy and pathetic.

The woman slapped her own forehead. 'I have a very big mouth—forgive me, I meant no harm. I didn't know you were serious about him.'

'I'm not.' Cara strove to affect nonchalance. From the pity in the other woman's eyes, she failed miserably at it.

'I must use the bathroom now,' the woman said, shuffling to the door. 'Please, forget what I said. I didn't know—'

'I'm not serious about him,' Cara interrupted, her horror at the woman's assumptions trumping her innate shyness. 'I'm well aware Pepe has the attention span of a goldfish.'

'That is a little unfair,' the woman said with a slight crease in her forehead. 'To goldfish.' With a quick wink she entered the bathroom and shut the door behind her.

Taking rapid breaths, Cara rejoined the party, trying desperately to contain the nerves that threatened to overwhelm her.

As she sought out Pepe she could feel people staring at her, feel their curiosity about this stranger in their midst. For this was no social-networking occasion, this was a proper party for friends to mingle, catch up on each other's lives, drink too much alcohol and behave indiscreetly. She couldn't even have a glass of wine to calm her nerves.

Eventually she found him chatting to a couple of women, a tall glass of beer in his hand. Walking towards them, she almost came to a stop when she saw one of the women cup his buttocks and give them a squeeze. How Cara's feet carried on moving, she had no idea, but it felt as if a million hot pins were being poked into her skin.

Pepe laughed and grabbed the wandering hand. He

brought it to his lips. Whatever he said as he kissed it made the wandering-hand woman burst into laughter.

'Cara,' he called, spotting her and beckoning her over. When she reached him, he placed an arm around her waist, his hand gripping her hip. The same hand that just moments earlier had held another woman's hand so he could kiss it.

'I don't think I've introduced you—this is Lena and Francesca. Ladies, this is Cara.'

The two women looked at her with unabashed interest. Wandering-hand lady held her hand out. Much as she wanted to refuse, Cara forced herself to shake it, all the while thinking, *This hand just squeezed Pepe's butt. This is* another *of his ex-lovers.*

How many of them were here?

The hot pins poking her skin were now strong enough to make her brain burn.

'Ladies, look after her for me while I get her a drink.' With that, Pepe disappeared into the crowd.

Francesca, the non-wandering-hand woman, an adorably plump blonde who had squeezed herself into a black dress that gave her a cleavage like two pillows, was the first to speak. 'I don't think we have met before, *non*?'

Cara shook her head.

'How did you come to meet Pepe?'

At least it was a question she could answer. Even so, it took two attempts for the words to form. 'His brother is married to my best friend.'

Francesca's eyes gleamed. 'Ah, Luca. Now that is one fine specimen of man,' she said, turning back to Lena.

The two Frenchwomen spoke in their native language before Lena addressed Cara. '*Je regrette un... non* English.'

'Lena doesn't speak English,' Francesca said apologetically. 'I am translating.'

Even if Cara had actually paid attention in her senior school French classes, there was no way she would have been able to keep up with the speed with which the two women spoke.

As Cara stood there like a spare wheel while the two women conversed loudly before her, that same dreadful outsider feeling doused her all over again.

'I need to find Pepe,' she whispered, backing away, horribly aware her cheeks were flaming.

Slipping back into the crowd, she spotted him easily enough, standing by the bar with what looked like a glass of orange juice in his hand. It came as no surprise to find him talking to a woman. This woman's hand was playing with the lapel of his tuxedo jacket.

If her brain could burn much more it would boil. Everything inside her felt taut, as if it had been wound into a coil. Perspiration broke out on her skin.

'Where are you going?' Pepe caught hold of her wrist as she passed him.

She hadn't even realised her legs were moving.

'To the bathroom.' She said the first thing that came into her mind.

'Again?'

'Yes.'

His eyes narrowed slightly as he studied her. 'You're very pale. Are you all right?'

'Yes.' She tugged her wrist out of his hold. 'Excuse me. I'll be back in a minute.'

The lapel-fingering woman said something to him in French, looking at Cara as she spoke. No doubt she too was asking if Cara was his latest lover. The latest in a long, long line.

Taking advantage of his momentary distraction, Cara slipped out of the door. This time the adjoining room was full of partygoers all talking and laughing loudly. A small queue had formed by the bathroom.

She didn't want the bathroom. She wanted to escape. She wanted to get as far away from Pepe and all the women who had shared his bed as she could.

As she stood there, feeling helpless, not knowing what to do, the opportunity for escape presented itself.

A door in the far corner flew open and a latecomer, dressed in a long coat and carrying a box of champagne, burst into the room. This was clearly someone who hadn't bothered to observe the rule of using the outside entrance.

Screams of laughter greeted the newcomer's entrance. Cara took her advantage and skirted her way past the crowd to the door.

Bingo.

The staircase was dimly lit and narrow, but she easily made her way down the first few flights until she reached the first floor. There, she shrank back to avoid a couple of bustling waitresses exiting large swing doors to the left, expertly carrying plates of steaming food.

Making sure no other member of the café staff was waiting to use the swing doors, she carried on to the ground floor and found herself in the centre of the café, right next to the bar.

A young man pouring a bottle of lager into a glass spotted her. *'Je vous aider?'* he said, openly appraising her.

Not having a clue what he'd just said, she grappled for the right words in a language she hadn't spoken in over a decade. *'Un téléphone, s'il vous plaît?'*

'Un téléphone?'

'*Oui. Je voudrais un taxi.*' She couldn't hide the desperation from her voice. '*S'il vous plaît.*'

He appraised her a little longer than was necessary before nodding. '*Une minute,*' he said, then left the bar and walked to a table where four middle-aged men were loudly slurping coffee. They all turned to look at her.

'Hey, English,' one of them called to her.

'Irish,' she corrected, inching closer to them.

'Need taxi?'

She hesitated before nodding. She might be desperate to get out of this place but she'd heard every horror story going about single women getting lifts with strange men.

He pulled a wallet out of his back pocket and showed her his ID, proving he wasn't a mad axeman as her hackles feared. He was a taxi driver.

'You have money?' he asked, no doubt referring to her lack of a bag or clutch.

'It's at the house,' she said, thinking of her precious forty-eight euros. She gave him the name of the street where Pepe lived.

He looked her up and down, no doubt estimating the cost of her silk dress before inclining his head and getting to his feet. 'Wait here. I get car.'

She cast a nervous glance over her shoulder to the direction of the staircase. It wouldn't be long before Pepe noticed she was missing.

Actually, with all those women fawning all over him, it was likely he wouldn't notice she'd gone for hours. All the same, she didn't want to take the risk.

If she was to see him now, she had no idea how she would react.

'Is it okay to pay you when we get there?'

He slipped his jacket on and shrugged.

Taking the shrug as assent, she followed him out into

the cold night air, hugging her arms round her chest and wishing she'd had the chance to grab her wrap, which had been whisked away as soon as they'd walked into the loft. The taxi was parked around the corner, but she made no attempt to soak up her surroundings, her entire focus on getting back to Pepe's house, getting her passport and getting the hell out of there.

The journey back passed in a blur. The only thing she saw on the entire journey was those women's hands touching Pepe as if they owned him.

When they arrived on Pepe's street, she got the driver to crawl along until she recognised his distinctive red front door.

'Give me a minute to get my money,' she said, turning the handle. And then God knew what she would do. The fee was thirty euros.

To her disquiet, the driver also got out of the cab and followed her up the steps to the front door.

She rang the bell. And rang it again. Then banged on it. Then rang it again, all the while aware of the driver standing beside her impatiently.

She banged one last time before she remembered— Monique didn't work weekends. Pepe had told her just a few hours ago that she would be returning to her own home.

Despair was almost enough for Cara to hit her head against the unyielding door.

Eejit that she was, she'd run away to an empty house for which she didn't have a key.

Swallowing away the bile that had lodged in her throat, she tried to think. Nothing came. Her mind was a complete blank.

She didn't have a clue what to do.

'I can't get into the house.'

'I want my money.' The driver's tone was amiable enough but she detected the underlying menace in it.

'You'll get it.' She rubbed a hand down her face. 'Give me your address. I'll drop it over to you as soon as Pepe gets home and lets me in. I'll sign anything you want.'

'You don't pay?'

'I will pay. But I can't get into the house, so I can't get my purse.'

'You don't pay, I get police.'

'No, please.' Her voice rose. 'I promise, I will pay it. I promise. I'm not a blaggard.'

A meaty hand grabbed her shoulder. 'You pay or I call police.'

Her fear rising, she tried to shake him off. 'I *will* pay. Please don't call the police.'

His hand didn't budge other than to lock onto her biceps. 'Come, we go see police.'

'Get off me!' she cried. All the heat in her skin had been replaced by cold terror. The thought of being dragged into a police station and being accused of criminality was more than she could bear.

But the driver was clearly furious and had no intention of letting her go. Keeping a tight grip on her, he hauled her back down the steps to the cab.

Before she could open her lungs to scream for help, a large car sped around the corner, coming to a stop before them in a screech of brakes. The engine hadn't been turned off before Pepe jumped out of the passenger side and took long strides towards them.

'Take your hands off her *now*,' he barked, his anger palpable.

'She no pay,' the driver said, refusing to relinquish his hold, even though he'd turned puce at the sight of Pepe.

'I *said*, take your hands off her. *Maintenant!*'

Before Cara knew what was happening, the driver let her go and a slanging match between the two men erupted, all of it conducted in French, so she couldn't keep up. Her hands covering her mouth, she got the gist of it well enough.

If she weren't witnessing it with her own eyes, she would never have believed Pepe was capable of such fury. The menace came off him in waves of pumped-up testosterone, his face a contortion of wrath.

It ended with Pepe pulling a wad of notes from his pocket and throwing them at the driver with a string of words spat at him for good measure. A couple of the said words jumped out at her as she recalled how she and Grace had once made it their mission to learn every possible swear word in French. She was pretty sure Pepe had just used the very choicest of those words.

When he finally looked at her, the rage was still there. 'Get in the house,' he said tightly, sweeping past her and up the steps, unlocking the door.

'What the hell do you think you're playing at?' He slammed the door shut behind her.

'I'd forgotten Monique had the night off. Thanks for coming to my rescue.' Her breaths felt heavy, the words dredged up. She knew she should show proper gratitude towards him—if Pepe hadn't arrived when he did she would likely be bundled in the back of the taxi on her way to the nearest police station. But now they were safely ensconced in his home, her fright had abated a little but blood still pumped through her furiously. Forget the driver, all she could see were those overfamiliar women and Pepe's amused, arrogant self-entitlement as he accepted their attentions.

'I thought he was trying to rape you.'

'Well, he wasn't.' She was barely listening. She kicked

her crystal shoes off. 'He was trying to get me to a police station to have me arrested.'

'What did you run off for? You told me you were going to the bathroom! You humiliated me in front of my friends.'

'Oh, poor diddums,' she said, making no effort to hide her sarcasm. 'I couldn't stomach staying at that party a minute longer.' Turning, she hurried through the reception and up the spiral staircase.

'Are you feeling ill?' He kept pace easily. Too easily.

'Yes. I feel sick. Sick, sick, sick.' She practically ran to her room.

'Why didn't you say something instead of running off and leaving me like a fool waiting for your return?'

'Because *you're* the cause of my sickness. Now get lost.' Thus said, she slammed the door in his face.

Immediately he shoved it back open. 'What the hell do you think you're doing?'

'Leaving.'

Uncaring that he stood mere feet away, and uncaring that the dress she wore cost thousands of euros, she tugged it off and threw it onto the floor, unceremoniously followed by her matching designer bra and knickers. The clothing felt soiled, bought to satisfy his conscience.

'Like hell you are.'

'Like you can stop me.' Storming into the walk-in wardrobe filled with yet more clothing bought to satisfy his conscience, Cara rummaged through until she found the dress she'd worn to the christening. Her dress. Bought with *her* money.

In the back of her mind a voice piped up telling her to clad herself in as much of the designer clothing as she could before leaving. It would be something to sell online.

She ignored it. Sanity could go to hell. These expensive clothes, as beautiful as they were, made her feel cheap.

She found her original underwear, freshly laundered, and stepped into the knickers.

'Where are you going to go?'

'Home.'

'How are you going to get there? You don't have any money.'

She turned on him. 'I don't know!' she screamed. 'I don't know where I'm going to go or how I'm going to get there, but as long as I'm far away from you I don't care!'

'If you walk away you will never see me or my money again. Your child will grow up without a father. Is that what you want?'

'Why would I want our child to know *you* as its father? You'd be a lousy father just as mine was. Selfish.'

'I am *nothing* like your father.'

'So you keep saying and, do you know what, I think you're right. My father might be an utter scumbag but even he wouldn't hold his own baby hostage as you're doing.'

'I'm doing no such thing,' he said, his own voice rising, a scowl forming on his face. 'I'm trying my best under difficult circumstances to protect our child.'

'By holding your bank account and the promise of access to it over my head as a sick method of keeping me prisoner? That'll be a good story to tell the grandkids.'

'I will do whatever is necessary to ensure my child makes it into this world without coming to harm.'

'My child? Our child? So you're admitting paternity now, are you?'

'No!' He swore. At least she assumed he swore, given the word he spurted out in Italian contained real vehemence behind it. 'It was a slip of the tongue.'

'You're good at that,' she spat with as much vehemence as *she* could muster.

'And what do you mean by that?'

'Only that you must have slipped your tongue into half the women at that party tonight. How many of your exes were there? A dozen? More?'

His eyes glittered with fury before the visible anger that had seemed to swell in him dissipated a touch.

He leaned back against the wall and surveyed her. 'You're jealous.'

Her response was immediate and emphatic. 'Don't talk such rot.'

'You are.' He said it with such certainty she tightened her grip on the bra lest she punch him one.

'I am not jealous!' How dared he even suggest such a thing? Jealous because of *him*? 'I was humiliated. All those women acting as if they owned you, all pretty much spelling out what a great lay you are... Is it any wonder it made me feel sick?'

'See?' A half-smile played on his lips. 'I knew you were jealous.'

'For me to be jealous would mean I have to have feelings for you, and the only feelings I have for you are hate. Do you understand that, Pepe? I despise you.'

Turning her back on him, she stormed into her en suite and locked the door behind her.

She absolutely was not jealous.

No way.

For the first time she realised she'd been screaming at him with only her knickers on. Could her humiliation get any greater?

She tried to put the bra on but her hands shook so much she couldn't hook it together. And she'd left her stupid dress in the room.

Pepe banged on the door.

'Go away!' she screamed. 'Just leave me alone.'

'I'm not going anywhere.'

'Well, I'm not coming out until you're gone.'

'Then you'll be in there for a long time. For ever, if necessary. Because I am not going anywhere.' Now there was no amusement to be heard in his voice. Only a determined grimness.

Let him wait. Let him wait for ever. Let him…

Patience was clearly not Pepe's forte. 'You have exactly ten seconds to open this door or I will break it down. Ten.'

The fight began to seep from her. This was all too much. 'Please, Pepe, just leave me alone.'

'Eight.'

He was serious.

'Seven.'

The tears that had been fighting to break free for the past hour suddenly escaped. She could no more contain them than she could prevent him breaking the door down.

'Four.'

With salt water rushing down her cheeks like a mini waterfall and trembling hands, she unlocked the door and pulled it open.

CHAPTER TEN

ALL THE ANGRY emotion raging through Pepe's blood constricted when he saw Cara standing there sobbing, still clutching her bra, only her knickers on to protect her nakedness.

Something hot and sharp pierced through his chest.

Instinct and something deeper, something unquantifiable, made him close the gap between them and wrap his arms around her.

'Shh,' he whispered, resting his chin on her cloud of hair and raising his eyes to the ceiling. 'Please don't cry, *cucciola mia.*'

She didn't even attempt to fight, just clung to him and cried into his chest, sobs racking her frame. Her generous breasts compressed against him but for once he couldn't react to it. Cara's sobs hurt his heart too much for him to care about anything but soothing them away.

He'd spent the past five days doing his best to forget she was pregnant. He'd been so set on blocking it out that he'd completely failed to take *her* feelings into account. Cara was such a feisty woman it was easy to forget her vulnerabilities. But she was vulnerable. Pregnancy made her more so.

He remembered the first time he'd met her. It seemed so long ago that it could have been a different lifetime but in truth it had only been a few years. It was a few weeks before his brother had married Grace. Cara had gone to stay with them in the build-up to the wedding and Luca had talked him into going on a double date, pointing out Cara would feel like a gooseberry otherwise. As she was such an important part of his bride-to-be's life, Luca was determined Cara would find Mastrangelo hospitality second to none.

Pepe hadn't been impressed. He'd been used to strong, confident women; the only bit of vivacity he'd found on Cara had been the colour of her hair. Other than that, she'd been like a wallflower, practically gluing herself to Grace's side, talking to him and Luca only when spoken to and even then in monosyllables. He'd thought her surly and rude.

As the wedding had approached, slowly he'd seen a different side to her unfurl, until, by the day of the nuptials, when he had been best man and she the chief bridesmaid, she was happy to chat with him as easily as she could with Grace.

But no one else.

He'd come to realise she wasn't surly, just painfully shy. It took her a while to overcome her nerves with someone, but when she did, she was excellent company with a dry wit that delighted him. But...she'd been Grace's best friend. She would likely always be a part of his life. There was a vulnerability to her that none of his lovers had. Any attraction to her was quashed.

He would not involve himself with vulnerable women, no matter how sexy they were. All the same, he'd enjoyed her company, would happily return home to Sicily when she stayed there and go out on double dates. They always had the best of times together.

He'd known early on from Grace's disappearance that

Cara would hold the key to finding her. But he'd put it off. And put it off some more, always hoping Grace would turn up of her own accord or that Luca would find another clue to finding her. But as the months had passed with no word, he could not in all conscience stand idly by while his brother turned into an emotional wreck. So he'd swallowed that same conscience and sought Cara out. The one woman he'd sworn he would never seduce…

He'd spent the best weekend of his life with her.

He'd been haunted by memories of it ever since.

And now she was here, back in his arms. Her naked breasts crushed against him. Breasts that tasted like nectar…

His blood thrummed, deep and heavy, his senses reacting to the scent and feel of *her*, a primitive desire that came alive only for her.

He did not want to admit those brief moments of fear when he'd realised she'd gone from the party. Vanished into the night.

He did not want to think of the cold tightness that had clutched at his chest as he'd forced his driver to put his foot down through the dark Montmartre streets.

He did not want to think of his rage when he'd seen that oaf of a taxi driver manhandling her in such a callous manner.

Pepe despised violence. He'd grown up surrounded by it, not in his family, but in the associations his father had had until *he* had allowed his own conscience to lead him away from it.

Growing up, Pepe had vowed he would never allow his fists do the talking for him. Even when he'd felt the hot blade of the knife slice down his cheek he hadn't retaliated. He'd been so numb from the preceding events that it had almost been a relief to feel something.

Yet for all that, it had taken every ounce of restraint not to throw himself onto the taxi driver and pulverise him.

If that driver had hurt her in any way, he doubted he'd have been able to hold on to that restraint.

Cara had stilled. He could feel her breath, hot through the crisp linen of his shirt, tickling his skin.

'I...I need to put some clothes on,' Cara said, trying to break away. It was happening again, that almost liquid feeling in her bones, the slavish desire creeping through her every pore. She tried to pull away but Pepe was too strong.

'You're not going anywhere.'

She hated the thrill that surged through her at his unequivocal declaration.

All she could see were his women. Her head was crowded with them, all lined up and merrily waving at her, happy—proud even—to be used by him and, she had to admit, use him in return. There was no romance. Romance had nothing to do with Pepe's liaisons.

Eejit that she was, she'd once been proud of her immunity to him.

It had been one big fat lie cooked up by her pride because he had never shown the slightest bit of interest in her other than as a friend. He'd flirted with her the same way he'd flirted with every other woman on his radar, but not once had he tried it on. Not until he'd needed something from her.

She'd been *happy* believing his sexual ambivalence towards her was mutual. She'd felt *safe*. Look at the trouble she'd got herself into when she'd allowed herself to believe otherwise.

She didn't feel safe now. Not pressed against his broad frame with his arms wrapped around her so protectively, his hand snaking down her naked spine, marking her, his musky scent filling her senses...

Her tears had left her feeling raw. Exposed and hollow. Except the void inside her was filling with something else that she tried desperately to stop. Heat. Sweet, sweet heat that pushed the tormenting images away, until the only thing that filled her head and the hollow ache inside her was *him*.

'Those women meant nothing to me.' His gravelly tones whispered into her ear, his breath warm, sending tiny darts of pleasure skittling across her skin.

Her breath hitched. 'And I do?'

He clasped her cheeks with his big hands, tilting her head back so she was forced to look at him. His eyes were deep pools of lava.

'I don't know what you mean to me,' he said, his honesty stark. Brutal. 'You've been in my head for four months and I can't shift you from there. If I'd had the choice, I would have wanted more than one night with you. And you would have wanted more than one night with me.'

Before she had the chance to form a lie of denial, his head tilted and his lips moulded on hers.

Her response was stark and utterly shocking. All the sweet heat swirling inside her immediately converged into a pool of need so deep the intensity frightened her. It took all her strength not to react, not to move her lips in time with his.

She wanted to punch at him, but when she moved her hands to his shoulders to push him away, her fingers gripped onto him.

Pepe's lips cajoled and teased and still she resisted, fighting with the last of her will power until his tongue broke through the tight line of her lips and darted into the heat of her mouth.

Something inside her snapped.

Her grip on his shoulders tightened as she responded in kind, exploring his mouth and sensuous lips as if his kisses were the life raft to cling to, to stop her drowning.

His hands caressed away from her cheeks, one snaking round to gather her hair together and spear her scalp— she had no idea when it had escaped the confines of the tight chignon—the other making broad strokes down her back until it reached her bottom. He clasped it and pulled her tight to him so his arousal was stark against her belly.

Pure, undiluted heat rushed through to her core and an unwitting moan escaped from her throat.

'*Cucciola mia,*' Pepe groaned, breaking away to nip at her delicate earlobe. Unbelievably, he was already fired up enough to explode.

Thank God he was still dressed. If he'd been naked, he would have plunged into her the second that earthy moan had echoed into his senses.

Drums played loudly in his head, his heart thundering to the same rhythm.

The bed was only a few feet away but the distance could be as far as the moon.

Unwilling to break away from her delectable body for more than the fraction of a moment, he shuffled her to the bed then gently pushed her onto it so she was sitting on the edge.

'Don't move,' he ordered, drinking her in, her colour-heightened cheeks, her bottom lip plump and begging to be kissed, her green eyes bright and dilated, her breasts heavy and swollen, the pale nipples ruched.

'*Sei bella,*' he said thickly. And she was. Beautiful.

Jeez, his hands were trembling, his fingers and thumbs

disconnected from his brain, unable to work the buttons on his shirt.

Abandoning his quest to undress himself, he sank to his knees before her and gripped her hips, pulling her to him so she looked down at him.

There she sat, gazing at him with a heavy desire he recognised and which filled him with something that fizzed in his heated blood. Her fiery hair hung down and he reached for a lock of it, greedily inhaling the sweetness of its scent.

He straightened a little to kiss her again, gratified beyond measure when she responded in kind, kissing him back, her tongue playing with his, mimicking his actions while her small hands gripped his scalp.

He covered one of her breasts with the palm of his hand, thrilling to feel the soft weightiness of it, and rubbed his thumb over the nipple. Cara arched her back in response and dug her nails into his skull, deepening their kiss.

These kisses, no matter how delicious and rousing they were, were not nearly enough.

He wanted to see if she responded with the same wild abandon that had caused him to lose his head four months ago.

But first he wanted to taste *all* of her.

Trailing kisses down her neck, he reached her breasts and hungrily took one puckered nipple into his mouth.

She moaned and cradled his scalp some more, pushing him against her. Lavishing attention on her other breast, he then bent down lower, raining kisses over the softness of her rounded stomach and down to the black lace covering the heart of her.

Hooking the side of her knickers with his fingers, he tugged at them, looking back up at her as he pulled them down to her ankles. He could smell her arousal, a scent that hit him like an aphrodisiac cloud.

'Spread your legs.' Did that thick guttural voice really belong to him?

Colour heightened her cheeks and, for one heart-stopping moment, he thought she would refuse.

'Please,' she said through heavy breaths, 'turn out the light.'

He kissed her. 'It will be good. I promise.'

Understanding her shyness, he did as she requested, turning out the main light so the only illumination came from the landing, then returned to kneel before her.

He placed a hand on a trembling thigh. 'Lie back,' he said thickly.

She swallowed, before leaning back, her eyes not leaving his face until he gently pushed her thigh to one side.

Cara's eyes closed and her head rolled back, her chest rising and falling rapidly.

Moving the other thigh to expose her to his covetous eyes, he held her open to him. Even in the dim light he could see the moisture glistening from her, her arousal there for him to see, and as he pressed his mouth to the heart of her he was suddenly grateful to still be clothed. Unable to relieve his own tension meant there was no danger of embarrassing himself by coming too soon.

Dimly he remembered being on their hotel bed in Dublin and her refusal to let him go properly down on her. He'd placed a simple kiss between her spread legs before she'd pushed him away and clamped her thighs back together.

He hadn't pressed her on it, had simply thought she was as eager as he for him to be inside her. He'd never considered that she could be a virgin who had never been naked in front of a man.

Now he realised he'd got off lightly. If he'd been given a real taste of her arousal then, he doubted he would have slept in four months.

Cara's scent and taste should be bottled as an aphrodisiac.

Her tiny moans deepened and when his tongue found her clitoris she jerked and gasped, tried to move him off her.

'Relax,' he murmured, pressing a hand to her belly while slowly inserting a finger inside her. If he didn't already know how aroused she was, this would have proved it beyond doubt.

Relax? Oh, how desperately she wanted to. How Cara yearned to let herself go and lose herself in the wonders of what Pepe was doing to her, because it felt *so good*.

But she couldn't.

No matter how hard she concentrated on the magic of his tongue and fingers, no matter how much her body ached for release, the switch in her brain refused to turn off and just let go.

'Please, Pepe,' she murmured when she could not take any more. 'Make love to me.'

He looked up at her with hooded eyes, a wolfish grin spreading over his face. 'Say it again.'

'I want…'

He got to his feet. For one fearful moment she thought he was going to leave her there, exposed on so many levels.

Instead he unbuttoned his shirt, his movements deft. He cocked an eyebrow. 'You want…?'

She swallowed moisture away, staring dazedly at the magnificence of his body as he shrugged the shirt off and casually discarded it.

His trousers and underwear quickly followed, and all she could do was gaze at him with a catch in her throat.

Pepe's arousal was all too apparent, his erection jutting out in front of him, large and proud.

'You want?' he repeated, stepping between her still-parted legs. 'I want to hear you say it. I want to hear from your own lips that you want this.'

She understood why he was demanding this from her and in a way she couldn't blame him. Even if she did blame him it would make no difference. If he were to walk away right now the big deep pool she was swimming in would dissolve into a tiny puddle. 'I want this. *I want you.*'

His eyes glittered. 'Then you shall have me.'

He leaned down over her, barely touching her, the dark silky hair on his chest brushing against her sensitised breasts, tickling her. Slanting his lips on hers, he kissed her with a possessiveness that took her breath away, his hands kneading her thighs until he had her exactly where he wanted her.

And then he was inside, joyously, massively, deeply inside her, filling her completely.

'Ahh,' she moaned, pulling him down so his full weight was on her, adjusting herself slightly to accommodate him further, to allow him even deeper penetration.

Her body remembered the heights he'd taken her to before and, like a greedy child, was desperate to feel those same sensations again, to experience the same rippling pleasure that had blown her mind.

In and out he thrust, kissing her, squeezing her breasts, clutching her hips, penetrating to her very core until she felt everything inside her tighten.

As if he could sense that she was on the edge, Pepe

increased the tempo and ground even deeper into her. It was enough.

Her orgasm rippled through her in waves so powerful and beautiful that any form of coherence abandoned her and all she could do was ride it, catching every last swell.

Cara awoke with a jolt.

An arm was curved around her belly. Deep, heavy breathing sounded from the pillow beside her.

Swallowing, she opened her eyes.

Pepe was there beside her, fast asleep. Through the dusky light she gazed at the thick black lashes, the dark stubble across his jawline, the mussed hair, the trimmed goatee.

Her heart constricted then began to hammer. She swallowed again.

After they had made love for a second time, Pepe had gathered her into his arms and fallen asleep with her head resting on his chest. Sleep had come easily for him.

She, on the other hand, had lain awake for an age. She'd disentangled herself from his arms knowing she should wake him and insist he return to his own room. Instead she'd found herself gazing at him, much as she was staring at him now. He was just so beautiful, even in repose with his mouth slightly parted, that firm yet sensuous mouth that had brought her such pleasure.

In this ethereal morning light she couldn't find the energy to rebuke herself for being so stupid as to fall back into his bed.

Recriminations could wait.

All she could focus on at that moment was that sensual mouth.

Slowly she brought her face to his, close enough to feel his breath against her skin. Closing her eyes, she brought her lips to his, breathing him in. She raised a hand to his face and gently traced her fingers down his cheek and down the strength of his neck and over his broad shoulders. It amazed her that a body so hard could be covered with skin so smooth.

Slowly she explored him, dragging her fingers through the silky hair on his chest, circling the dark brown nipples, then tracing down the flat hardness of his belly. Her pale hand contrasted against the darkness of his olive skin. They were a couple full of contrasts, her yin to his yang.

Not that they were a couple, she reminded herself hastily. They were simply two individuals thrown together by circumstances with a chemistry that refused to be denied. If not for the life growing inside her, Cara would not be here. Pepe would likely not be here either, or if he was it would be in the arms of another.

Her stomach curdled at the thought and she squeezed her eyes shut to banish it.

Was that what her mother had done? How many times had *she* squeezed her eyes shut to banish the pictures of her husband with his other women?

Before the images could swamp her, Pepe's eyes opened and fixed on her, bringing her back to the here and now.

'You stopped,' he murmured, his voice thick with sleep. She hadn't realised her hand had stopped its exploration until he enfolded it with his own.

All memories dissolved as he pulled her down for a kiss, breathing in heavily.

Returning it, she closed her eyes and allowed him to guide her hand down to the thick mass of hair on his groin and the erection that had sprung from it.

Tentatively she encircled it, heat surging through her

as she felt its silky weight and length, felt it throb beneath her touch. When she rubbed her thumb over the tip she discovered the bead of moisture already there and felt a thrill like no other that this was for her. Even if it was only for now.

CHAPTER ELEVEN

WINTER SUN SHONE brilliantly through a gap in the heavy drapes right in Cara's eyes, waking her. She turned her head. Pepe had gone.

On legs that felt weighted, she climbed out of bed and padded over to the window, pulling the drapes open.

The room smelt of a familiar scent that she recognised from four months earlier. Sex. Their sex.

Air. That was what she needed. And plenty of it.

Firstly wrapping herself in the kimono, she unlocked the French door and stepped out onto the small balcony overlooking a large park.

The cold air hit her and she accepted it into her lungs, willing the frigid particles to douse her shame.

It did nothing of the sort.

She knew she didn't deserve to have her shame extinguished.

After everything she had been through and all the promises she had made her unborn child, she was no better than her mother.

Every time one of her father's affairs had come to light, which was a regular occurrence, her mother would vow to leave. Every time she changed her mind, too hooked on the highs and lows of her marriage to care about anything as basic as self-respect. Certainly too hooked to care about the effect it was having on her only child.

Her mother had been an addict. Her husband had been her fix. Not even his litter of illegitimates had made any difference.

And now here Cara was, well over a decade after her parents' marriage had finally done them all a favour and disintegrated, and she knew that unless she did something right now she would turn into an addict just as her mother had been.

Movement behind her caused her to turn.

Pepe stepped onto the balcony carrying two steaming mugs and wearing only a pair of faded jeans. There was something about seeing his feet bare that tugged at her in a manner that was entirely different from the effect his bare torso had on her.

'Good morning, *cucciola mia*,' he said with a lazy grin, handing her one of the mugs. Placing his own mug on the small table, he stood behind her and wrapped his arms around her waist, nuzzling into her neck.

'Please, don't,' she murmured, shaking her head. 'One accident with scalding tea is enough for anyone in a lifetime.'

He chuckled. 'In that case, drink up and we can go back to bed.'

She took a deep breath, planning to confess that she didn't want to go back to bed. Or, rather, that she did want to go back to bed with him. But she wanted it too much. That was the problem. She wanted it far too much.

Before she could speak he pressed a kiss into the small of her back then stood beside her at the balustrade.

'I owe you an apology,' he said, his light tone becoming serious. 'I'd forgotten how shy you are around strangers. I shouldn't have left you alone with anyone but me last night, not until I knew you were comfortable with them.'

Cara blinked in shock.

An apology was the last thing she'd expected to hear from Pepe's mouth.

She took a sip of her tea, determinedly looking out to the park, at the distant people walking their dogs, some carrying the morning's newspapers, life going on blithely regardless of her personal torment.

'I also should have warned you that a few of my ex-lovers would be there, but to be honest I never gave it a thought,' he continued. 'It's never been an issue. I should have taken into account that you are made from a different mould from them.'

The mention of his *ex-lovers* pierced like a lance into her skin. She forced herself to breathe, focusing on the park before her, allowing her attention to be captured by a young couple out for a bike ride, a toddler-sized child sitting in a special seat attached to the father's bike.

Pepe would never be a father in the traditional sense. He was too…free. Meeting his friends and the casual, bohemian intimacy they all shared had only confirmed everything she already knew.

And she, Cara, was of a *different mould*.

It hurt to admit it, but he was right. She could never be like those women. The scars of her childhood ran too deep. She could never share the man she loved. Just thinking of Pepe sharing intimacies with another woman made her skin go clammy and nausea swell inside her, and she didn't even love him.

Did she?

No, of course she didn't. Pepe might be able to reduce her to a quivering pulse of sensation but that didn't mean she was falling in actual love with him.

Did it?

'I need to leave,' she said, blurting the words out.

Whatever her feelings for him and whatever they meant, nothing could come of them.

Pepe stilled then cast an unreadable eye on her before getting his coffee. When he rejoined her at the balustrade he stood a good foot away from her.

'I'm going to appeal to your better nature to do the right thing and give me some money now so I can return to Dublin and find a home to raise our child in.'

'And if I don't?'

'Then I guess I'll have no choice but to stay. I know I was going to leave last night but I was so…' she almost said *devastated* '…upset that I wasn't thinking straight. I guess my hormones were playing up too, making every-thing seem ten times worse than it really was.'

Her hormones had had nothing to do with it. The white-hot jealousy she had experienced at the party had been all her own. She would rather chop her own ears off than admit it.

She took a deep breath before continuing. 'Even if I had been able to leave last night I would probably have come back like a dog with its tail between its legs. Noth-ing's changed. I'm still skint. My return ticket from Sicily is worthless here, so I have no way to get home until my wages from the auction house get paid into my account. But, Pepe, I can't stay here, especially not now.'

For the first time since joining Cara on the balcony, Pepe felt the chill of the air. He stared ahead at a young family who had been enjoying a bike ride. The parents had now dismounted and rested their bikes against a large tree, the father in the process of getting the toddler out of its seat.

Once he had dreamt of him and Luisa having such a family, had allowed his hopes and dreams to fill.

'Why are you so keen to get away from me?' he asked bitingly. 'Did I not satisfy you enough last night?'

'No, it was wonderful,' she said wistfully.

'Then what is the problem with staying here and sharing my bed?'

'Because we both know it won't be for ever. Chances are you'll be sharing it with someone else long before our baby is born.'

Imagining someone else in his bed drew a blank. It had drawn a blank since Dublin.

Until he and Cara were able to work through this strange desire that burned between them, he had the most sickening feeling he would never be able to move on.

'And what about you?' he asked more harshly than he would have liked. Something akin to panic was nibbling at his chest. 'How do I know you'll take care of yourself? How do I know you'll do what's right and what's best for the life inside you?'

He heard her take a sharp inhalation, but when she finally spoke her tone was a lot softer than he had been prepared for. 'What happened, Pepe? What happened to turn you into such a cynic that you believe me capable of harming our defenceless child?'

'Because it's happened to me before.'

He could feel Cara's eyes on him, could feel her shock. He kept his own eyes firmly fixed on the family in the distance. He had no idea where the parents had produced a ball from, but they were playing a game of what looked to be catch with their small toddler.

'I've not always been a cynic. I once believed in love and marriage. I was going to marry my childhood sweetheart.' He wasn't aware of the pained sneer that crossed his face. 'Once, just once, we failed to use contraception and Luisa fell pregnant. I was eighteen and she was seventeen.'

He could feel Cara's eyes still resting on him, took a small crumb of comfort that she didn't immediately start peppering him with questions.

His throat felt constricted. This was something he had never discussed before, not with Luca, not with anyone. But he owed Cara the truth, because somewhere, hidden deep inside him, was the knowledge that it *was* his baby she carried, a truth he dared not utter in case, by saying the words, it brought the whole thing crashing down.

'I was delighted at the prospect of becoming a father. I was…' He shook his head at the memory. 'At the time, my head was all over the place. My father had just died from a heart attack and I didn't know how to handle it. But then Luisa told me she was pregnant and suddenly there was proof that life *did* have meaning and that miracles did occur. Luisa and I had spoken of marriage many times and, to me, it made sense to just bring the whole thing forward. I wanted our child to be born a Mastrangelo with parents who shared the same name.'

Trying to collect his thoughts, he finished his now cold and tasteless coffee and finally allowed himself to look at Cara.

She stood with her back to the balustrade, her arms folded across her chest, staring at him.

His heart expanded to see the paleness of her cheeks and the undeniable apprehension ringing in her green eyes.

'I thought Luisa was happy too but as the weeks passed she became more and more withdrawn, refusing to let me tell my family or her family about the baby until the time was right. And then, the morning after the first scan, the day she had agreed we could tell the world of our joy, she confessed that she'd had a one-night stand. She'd slept with someone else while I'd visited Luca at his university for a weekend.' Now he didn't bother hiding his bitterness. 'She and her lover had forgotten to use contraception. She was so terrified I would find out she engineered things so that days later we too got so carried away we forgot to use contraception. That way, if she fell pregnant, she could pass the child off as mine.'

A low whistle escaped from Cara's lips. There was no apprehension in her eyes now. Only compassion. Which somehow made him feel worse.

'The only reason she confessed was because she couldn't live with the guilt.'

'What did you do?' Cara breathed.

He laughed cynically and shook his head. 'I said I didn't care. I told her it didn't matter. I told her I loved her enough that I would raise the child as my own even if there was doubt that it was mine. But that was a lie—it wasn't *her* I loved enough to do that for, it was my unborn child. Because that baby was *mine*. I had already committed my heart to it. I had pictured the boy or girl it would be, the teenager he or she would grow into. I had pictured walking my daughter down the aisle and I had imagined my grown son asking me to be his best man.'

Long-buried unspoken memories threatened to choke him but Pepe forced himself to finish his sordid story. 'At first she agreed. Then, a couple of weeks later, when she was fifteen weeks pregnant, she went away for a weekend to visit an aunt. That too was a lie. She had in fact gone to the UK for an abortion. Her lover—who, it

transpired, she was still seeing—had given her the money
to pay for it all.'

Silence hung between them, the air thick and heavy.

'Dear God,' Cara whispered. 'I am so sorry.'

'Sorry for what?' he snarled, his attempts to keep a
leash on his emotions snapping. 'That I was deceived?
That I was stupid enough to want to be cuckolded and
by Francesco Calvetti of all people…'

'*He* was her lover?'

'You know him?'

She shook her head and curled her lip in distaste. 'I
know *of* him.'

Of course she did. Luca, his brother, had gone into
business with the bastard, an association that had re-
cently ended. Grace, his sister-in-law, despised the man.
'When we were kids our parents used to force us to play
together. He and my brother were once good friends.'

Cara placed a tentative hand on his arm. He guessed
it was supposed to be a comforting gesture, but at that
moment comfort was the last thing he needed. He felt
too unhinged for that. Spilling his guts for the very first
time was not the catharsis people claimed.

He especially didn't want comfort from her, the woman
who made him feel more unhinged than he had felt in
fifteen years.

Enfolding her hand, he raised it to his cheek and
placed it on his scar. 'Luisa gave me this scar. I was so
angry at what she'd done, I called her every nasty, vin-
dictive and demeaning name I could think of. In return
she slashed me with a knife from her mother's kitchen.
I've kept the scar as a reminder never to trust.'

Cara's eyes were huge and filled with something that
looked suspiciously like tears.

He dropped her hand. 'So now you know it all. I hope

you can now understand why I do not trust people and why I cannot give you the money you want, not until after our baby is born. It's not personal towards you. Please believe that.'

Cara dressed mechanically in a blue skirt, black roll-neck jumper and a pair of thick black tights, and tied her hair back into a loose ponytail. Her hands shook, her mind filled with him, with Pepe.

After their talk on the balcony he had disappeared, muttering about needing a swim. Wordlessly she had let him go, too shocked and heartsick at his story to even attempt to stop him.

Her heart stopped when she found him in the kitchen eating a *pain au chocolat*. He'd added a black T-shirt to his jeans, his black hair was damp and he'd had a shave.

He lifted his eyes to see her standing hesitantly in the doorway, and got to his feet. 'Please, help yourself,' he said, indicating the plate heaped with pastries in the centre of the table. 'I've made a pot of tea for you.'

Knowing he had gone out of his way to make the tea especially for her kick-started her heart. When he moved with fluid grace to pour a cup out for her and she spotted his bare feet, she had to blink back the sting of hot tears that burned in the backs of her eyes.

She reached for a plain croissant and placed it on the plate he'd laid out for her, then took the seat next to him. She broke a bit of it off and popped it into her mouth, all the while watching as he added milk to her cup before placing it before her.

'Thank you,' she whispered, breaking off another piece of croissant and nibbling at it. She wanted to touch him. She wanted to place her hands on his cheeks and kiss him.

'Do you know what I love the most about Grace?' she asked him when he'd sat back down.

He cocked an eye.

'Nothing. I love *everything* about her. When I moved to England at thirteen and started a new school, I was cold-shouldered by practically everyone. They all had their cliques. I was the outsider. But Grace took me under her wing. She would drag me into the art room at lunch breaks. She would drag me to parties at weekends and stay right by my side, making sure everyone included me. She introduced me to art. Even when it was obvious that I couldn't draw much more than matchstick men, she never put me down. I ended up practically moving into her home. She encouraged me to study History of Art at university because she could see that's where my passion lay. We studied different courses but we lived together and remained inseparable. I would give my life for Grace. She was more than a best friend. She was the one person who believed in me. My parents were so wrapped up in themselves they didn't care about me other than on the level of feeding and clothing me.'

Cara kept her gaze on Pepe as she spoke. If he could lay his soul bare then so could she.

'My father had so many affairs I lost count. Time after time, Mam would say she was leaving but every time she forgave him.' She shuddered. 'I would hear them having make-up sex. It was the most disgusting sound I've ever heard. Do you know what the worst part was?'

He shook his head, his face a mask.

'*He* left *her*. After all the affairs, the lies and the humiliation, one day he went to work and never came back. He'd found a teenage lover who "made him feel like a young man again". My mother was utterly devastated. I don't think she would ever have left him. She held on for two years in the hope that he would come back to her, but when he served her with divorce papers she finally accepted it was over and carted me off to England to start over.'

She popped the last of the croissant into her mouth. Unable to resist any longer, she stroked a hand down his smooth cheek and rubbed her thumb over the thick bristles on his chin. His deep blue eyes, which hadn't left her face, dilated, and his chest rose.

'Not long after we arrived in England, my mam started a new relationship with a man who was just like my dad. An unfaithful charmer. Everyone loves him but he is incapable of keeping his pecker in his trousers. And just like with my dad, she forgives him every time. I've spent my entire life feeling second best to my parents' libidos and hormones, and I'm terrified of turning out like them. Our child will *never* feel second best. Ever. I won't let it happen. Our child is innocent and deserves all the love I—and hopefully you—can heap on him or her.' She bit her lip. 'But, Pepe, I'm so *scared*.'

'Scared of what?'

'You,' she answered starkly. 'Until I met you, sex to me was tawdry and meant nothing but power and humiliation. I wanted none of it. But now I can understand why my mam let my dad treat her like a piece of rubbish and why she lets my stepdad treat her the same way, because I can feel it happening inside me when I'm with you. I woke up this morning and I knew I should leave but I was almost helpless to resist you. I'm scared that if I stay much longer I'll never want to go.'

CHAPTER TWELVE

PEPE COVERED CARA'S HAND, his eyes boring into her. 'Do you think you're falling in love with me?'

'No!' Her denial was immediate. Snatching her hand away, she wrung her fingers together on her lap and looked away.

'Good.'

She flinched.

He placed a finger under her chin and forced her to look up at him. 'I say "good" because there is a way to get through this without screwing either of us up. And without screwing up our child. I have never cheated on anyone in my life. After what Luisa did to me, it is not something I would ever put anyone else through. I like my affairs short and sweet. I admit, there are occasions when I will sleep with an ex, but never if either of us are involved with someone else.'

Pepe watched as she bit into her bottom lip. Learning the full truth of Cara's past explained so many things about her. His complaints about his own childhood seemed unbelievably petty in comparison. He'd never doubted his family's love for him.

'I have a proposal for you,' he said, thinking aloud. 'Will you hear me out?'

With obvious apprehension, she jerked her head.

'Let's see if we can make this work. We don't love each other but we do have a serious case of lust. Eventually it will work its way out of our systems.'

'Do you think?' She looked so hopeful he felt an incomprehensible stab of pain in his chest.

He nodded. 'For as long as we're together I can promise you exclusivity. Your mother lived in a vicious cycle of high emotion and denial, neither of which applies to us. We'll take it all one day at a time. When our desire for each other reaches its natural conclusion, we can go our separate ways—and hopefully we can go our separate ways as friends. We both want what's best for our child and that's for him or her to have parents who respect each other and can work together for their child's happiness. Our child will have two parents who are happy in themselves and have no antagonism towards the other.'

'So you do believe the baby is yours?'

He closed his eyes before inclining his head. 'Yes, *cucciola mia*. I believe the baby is mine.'

Pepe waited for a beat, just in case the world did come crashing down.

'Forgive me. Not trusting people is so hardwired into me that when you told me you were pregnant I went into denial. I think maybe I lost my head a little.'

'Make that a lot,' she said with a smile that lightened her features and lifted his spirits.

Cara was not Luisa. If there was one thing he knew about his flame-haired lover it was that she didn't have a selfish bone in her body. He could not in all good conscience make her continue to pay for Luisa's sins. And nor could he allow his child to pay.

His child.

He really was going to be a father.

His chest swelled with an emotion so pure it pushed all the oxygen from his lungs.

His child.

Their child.

'I think we should both promise to give this…thing a minimum of a fortnight to at least try and make it work.'

'No more being kept as a prisoner?'

'You are free to come and go as you please—I'll even give you your own set of keys. See, I *am* trying.'

'Very,' she agreed with a straight face.

He tapped her snub nose playfully, his spirits lifting even further. This could really work…

'If you give me your bank details I will deposit a sum of money into it which should go some way to recompensing you for your future loss of earnings with the auction house.'

'You do believe I'm not after your money?' she asked, suddenly looking anxious. 'All I want is for our child to be provided for.'

'And it will be,' he promised. Now that he had openly acknowledged his paternity it felt as if a great weight had lifted from him.

Deep inside, he had always known the truth. Cara was too…straight to tell anything but the most innocuous of lies. It was his own damaged pride that had refused to believe it.

A wave of something that felt suspiciously like guilt rolled into his guts.

He'd done the best he could, he told himself defiantly. Anyone who walked in his shoes would have reacted in the same way.

All the same, he knew he would have to go a long way to make it up to her.

And he knew the best way to start.

Reaching for her hips, he pulled her so she was sitting astride him.

'What are you doing?' she asked with a gasp.

'Celebrating our agreement.' Thus said, he tilted his head and kissed her.

'So this is how we celebrate?' she said when they finally came up for air.

He nuzzled into her neck, marvelling at the softness and the oh-so-heady scent. He was reminded of the way she had tasted on his tongue, could almost taste it anew. 'Can you think of a better way?'

She tilted her head back to give him better access and sighed. 'No. Nothing better. This is perfect.'

A fortnight came and went. It didn't even cross Cara's mind to leave.

Now that she was no longer a prisoner, life in general improved considerably. She could come and go as she pleased. She spent hours wandering around Paris's famous museums and galleries, including three days back-to-back at the Louvre, and spent many a happy lunch doing nothing but hanging out in Parisian cafés drinking hot chocolate.

Her personal belongings, including all her beloved art and history books, had finally been shipped over from Dublin and she had a marvellous time going through all her stuff. Most of it was put back in the boxes—she reminded herself on a daily basis that this was only a temporary arrangement and that it would not do to start thinking of it as permanent.

All the same, life with Pepe was good. More than good. Now that they had reached an understanding, all the antagonism had died. She knew that whatever happened between them, their child would not suffer for it.

He treated her like a princess. They'd gone for her twenty-week scan together, and to witness the adoration on his face was almost as thrilling as seeing her baby for herself. The money he'd put into her account—an amount that, if she were a cartoon character, would have made her eyes pop out of her head—had been happily spent that morning on baby furniture and other paraphernalia, with more than a little change left over. It was all now being stored in Pepe's humongous garage alongside his fleet of sports cars.

And now, back at the house, they were having a swim together in Pepe's underground luxury pool. Or, rather, she was lazing in the shallow end watching him swim lengths. He sped through the water like a porpoise, his strokes long and practised. There was something rather hypnotic about watching him, she mused. Who needed a book when one could watch Pepe?

After she'd counted him do approximately fifty lengths, he waded over to her, a large grin on his face. 'You should swim, lazybones.'

'I was admiring the view.'

His grin broadened and he swooped in for a kiss.

'Hmm,' she sighed, greedily kissing him back. It never ceased to amaze her how much Pepe wanted her. Or how much she wanted him. Already she could feel the stir of an erection in his swimming shorts, rubbing against her thigh.

'I've been thinking,' she said as he nuzzled into her neck, 'that I should really look at getting a driver's licence for when the baby's born.'

He stilled a touch. 'I can provide you with a car and a driver.'

'I'm sure you can,' she agreed drily. 'But it would be

nice to have the freedom to just…go, when the mood takes me.'

She had to think practically. She just had to. Thinking in detail about her and their baby's future kept her silly emotions in check. And if ever her stomach rolled at the thought of their future being without Pepe, she quashed it. After all, Pepe would always be an enormous part of their lives; they'd just be living under different roofs.

For the time being, things between them were magical, but she would *not* allow herself to think it could last for ever. Pepe didn't do for ever.

'Have you thought about where you'll want to live with the baby?' he asked, reading her mind.

'I was thinking maybe here in Paris,' she admitted. In the month they'd been together she'd travelled with him to his homes in Portugal and Spain. Of all the places Pepe called home, Paris was her favourite. There was something so wonderful about the city, the bustle, the chic women, the architecture, the art. Wandering the streets always evoked a feeling of contentment that was only surpassed at night when she would lie sated, wrapped in his arms, drifting off to sleep.

'Really? That's a great idea.' And it *was* a great idea, Pepe told himself. His stomach hadn't really cramped at the thought of Cara and their baby living away from him.

'It just makes sense, especially as this house is going to become your main base. It'll make it easier for the baby to be living in the same city as her mam and dad.'

He forced a smile. 'I was thinking of turning your old room into a nursery.'

'An excellent idea. You'll be right next to him or her then.' Her face scrunched. 'You'll have to move my boxes into another room though, at least until I move out.'

'Not a problem.' For practicality, they'd moved her

clothes and toiletries into his room, but all her other stuff was still in her old room, still in boxes from when he'd had it flown over from Dublin.

Cara was saying words that should have been balm to his ears. She'd not developed feelings for him that ran beyond a sexual level, and nor had she dropped any hints, subtle or otherwise, about making things between them permanent. Everything was proceeding exactly as planned. He was positive that any day soon his lust for her would start to abate. Any day.

So why did the thought of her living under a different roof from him make his chest feel so tight? Why did the thought of living without her make it hard to breathe?

After a long weekend in Sicily with Pepe's family, spent hanging out with Grace and deflecting her friend's worries about Cara and Pepe's relationship, Pepe left for a week-long trip to Chile, a distance they'd agreed was too far for her pregnant self to accompany him.

Alone in the house, Cara's mind kept drifting back to the talk she'd had with Grace, when her friend had tentatively voiced her concerns.

'Cara, you do know Pepe isn't a man for the long term? It's just that there's been no mention of marriage or anything—'

'Of course it's not permanent,' Cara had interrupted. 'We're just taking it a day at a time until it runs its course.'

'Do you know what you're doing?' Grace had asked with a furrowed brow.

'Of course I do,' she'd said defiantly. 'I'm getting to know my child's father properly. We're not going to have some fake marriage for the sake of the baby which only ends in misery for everyone. When our relationship runs its course we'll still be friends, which will only benefit our child. We don't want him or her being born into a war zone.'

She'd ignored her friend's worried face, pushed the image away now as she cast her eye around the huge space that was Pepe's living room.

Before leaving for Chile he had taken her to the huge vault storing his infamous art collection. 'I'm putting the hanging and placement of my collection in your hands,' he'd said solemnly.

Cara had been incredibly touched.

Pepe had left his multimillion-euro art collection in *her* hands, giving her carte blanche to hang and place them in his home as she saw fit. Trusting her.

Deciding where to place it all, overseeing the hanging— he'd insisted on getting professionals in because he didn't want her having to climb up and down stepladders when she was six months pregnant—had fulfilled her more than she had thought possible. It had been a project and a half, and one she had embraced with all the Irish enthusiasm that flowed in her blood.

Pepe had such an amazing and eclectic eye for art. Among the Old Masters were more modern pieces, including several by Georges Ramirez, one of which was a nude bronze whose torso she would recognise with her eyes closed using only her hands. The face was a blank but she would bet Pepe had been the model for it.

The only piece she disliked was the Canaletto. It brought back too many bad memories, serving as a reminder that Pepe could be ruthless when it came to getting what he wanted. She'd stuck that particular painting in a small guest room, all two million euros of it.

'Cara?'

Pepe's deep voice rang out from downstairs.

Quashing the urge to skip down the stairs to greet him, Cara forced her legs to move in a more sedate fashion.

'I'm right here,' she said, unable to hide the beam that spread over her face at the sight of him. It was the longest they had been apart and, despite the task he'd set her, she'd missed him dreadfully. Especially at night. The bed had felt empty without him. She would never admit it, lest he read too much into it, but on the second night she had given in and borrowed one of his shirts to sleep in.

After a long, knee-trembling kiss from him, she took his hand to give him the tour.

'Wow,' he said with open admiration as they stood in the main living area. 'You really know your stuff.'

Pepe was the first to admit he didn't know the first thing about art. The pieces he bought were never about investment—although that played a part in it—but were simply pieces that caught his eye and pulled at him.

Cara's own eye had placed them all exactly where they should be, the items selected for each room complementing the feel and décor of that particular room.

He'd smiled to see the portrait his sister-in-law had done of him hanging on the wall of his office. Grace had painted him as a Greek god but with a definite touch of irony and not a little humour.

'Are you happy to have that there, where anyone can see it?' Cara said, indicating the bronze by Georges Ramirez, which she had placed in the corner of the living room.

'You recognise it?' he asked wickedly.

'Of course I do,' she said with a frown.

With a jolt he realised she'd been living with him for two months. She knew him far more intimately than any other living person.

When, he wondered, would her allure no longer affect him?

He'd assumed they'd stay together for a few weeks, maybe a month, before he'd get her out of his system. He'd suggested a minimum of a fortnight, more to convey his sincerity in wanting to make things work between them than in any real hope.

Two months on and they were still together and he wanted her every bit as much as he had at the beginning. More so, if that was possible.

'Have you considered doing this professionally?' he asked, waving his hands around the room. 'I know plenty of people who would pay a small fortune to have their art collections displayed to their very best.'

'Not really,' she said with a shrug. 'Before Grace married Luca we often said we'd like to open our own gallery—she'd do all the art and I'd run it. But life takes over. I was very happy at the auction house.'

'Speaking of galleries, we've got a few hours to kill before we go to the exhibition tonight,' he said, referring to the opening of an up-and-coming new artist's work he'd promised they would attend. 'Shall we go for a swim?'

She pulled a face. 'My bikini line hasn't been done for weeks.'

'So? It's only me who's going to be looking.' He would be doing a lot more than looking. He'd be doing a lot more right now but for Monique bustling around in the kitchen, liable to barge into the living room at any moment.

A whole week without Cara had felt interminably long.

'I'd still feel self-conscious.'

'I can do it for you.'

Cara didn't trust the gleam that came into Pepe's eyes. 'Do what?'

'Your bikini line.'

'No way.'

'Why not?'

'Because…' Because she still wasn't comfortable with him being *down there*. Blame it on her Catholic upbringing—which was an irony in itself—or blame it on her reaching the grand old age of twenty-six before getting naked with a man, but, whatever the reason, she had a hang-up about her nether regions. Not Pepe's though. She adored *his* nether regions.

He arched an eyebrow. 'Because?'

She was stumped for a good answer.

She was still stumped for a good answer fifteen minutes later, sitting naked on a towel on the sofa in Pepe's bedroom.

'Relax, *cucciola mia*,' he purred, kneeling before her, having placed a jug of hot water on the floor beside him. He also carried a couple of razors and a tube of shaving gel. To make her feel less self-conscious he'd stripped off too. Or so he'd said.

'I need you to spread your legs,' he said, pouring some gel onto his palm.

Swallowing, she did as she was bid and parted her thighs.

'Further.'

She took a deep breath and exposed herself to him, resting her head back in a futile attempt to do as he'd suggested and *relax*.

'I won't hurt you,' he said with the utmost sincerity, before planting a kiss on her inner thigh. 'Trust me.'

Mixing the gel on his palm with a couple of droplets of the hot water, he rubbed his hands together to form a lather, then carefully swiped it over her bikini line, taking great care around the delicate area.

She closed her eyes. Happy to wax her legs, she'd always drawn the line at waxing her bikini area, preferring the less painful route of shaving.

Never in a million years would she have believed she'd allow someone else to do it for her.

When she finally dared look, she found his head bowed in concentration.

Trust me, he'd said.

With a jolt of her heart she realised that she *did* trust him.

She trusted him as she'd never trusted anyone other than Grace.

But this was a different form of trust. This was a deeper, more intimate trust, a trust she'd never expected to find with a man, with anyone.

'Okay?' Pepe's dark blue eyes were looking up at her.

She nodded and gave a half-smile. Her legs and torso were no longer tensed; indeed, her entire body had now relaxed.

'What do you think about Charlotte for a girl?' she said.

He looked up briefly, his lips pursing the way they always did when he was considering something. They'd already agreed on Pietro for a boy, in honour of Pepe's father. Choosing a girl's name had proved trickier. At first she'd thought he was being deliberately awkward when he dismissed the names she kept coming up with… until the penny dropped that he was, in his own subtle fashion, trying to avoid naming their child after any of his ex-lovers. Not all the names, thank God. A few he dismissed for other reasons, like thinking a particular name was 'wet'.

She'd now taken to throwing a name at him, watching him purse his lips and then shake his head, all the while hoping she never came across one of his 'friends' who shared that particular name.

This time, there was no shake of the head. Instead, a broad grin spread across his handsome face. 'That is perfect.' He nodded, still grinning. 'Charlotte Mastrangelo-Delaney. *Sì*—perfect.'

When he refocused his attention to his current handiwork, Cara tried to shake away the jealousy coursing through her blood, knowing she was being irrational. So what if Pepe had been prepared to marry Luisa so they and their child could all share the same surname? In those days he'd been little older than a child himself with romantic ideals that had no place in the real world.

Cara and Pepe had reached the perfect compromise when it came to naming their child, both reasoning that it wasn't his baby, or her baby, but *their* baby, and therefore should share both their names.

At least he was capable of compromise. Most of the time. He still had an unerring ability to get his own way on most things. Like now.

Before much more time elapsed, he leaned back and flashed a grin. 'See—that wasn't too bad, was it?'

'It was fine.'

'Stay where you are—I need to get some fresh water to clean you up.'

She watched him stride off to the en suite, not in the least bothered about his nudity, with a lump in her throat. No wonder so many artists clamoured to immortalise him in whatever medium they used. Pepe's strength and poise, mixed with his underlying good humour, were like nectar to a bee.

He returned with a fresh jug of water and a towel.

This time he didn't have to ask her to part her legs.

'Have you done this lots of times?' she asked, then

immediately castigated herself. His answer had the potential to lance her.

His eyes met hers, glittering with something she didn't recognise. 'Never.'

Her heart hitched.

For long moments neither moved. She wished she could read what was swirling in his eyes, but before she could catch it, he broke the hold.

Bowing his head, he placed a kiss on the area he'd just shaved. Then another kiss. And another.

His movements were so gentle and…reverential, that as he made his way to the very heart of her she forgot to feel embarrassed, lying back to rest her head on the back of the sofa and simply *feel*.

Pepe was such a wonderful lover, she thought dreamily. So tender yet so fantastically wild, and always wanting her. She remembered how he'd arrived back from an overnight stay in Germany. Within five minutes of getting home he'd had her bent over on the desk in his study. She'd been so desperate for him too that they'd been like a pair of rutting animals.

Heat from these gorgeous memories pooled into her core right at the moment Pepe found her clitoris. She moaned.

Her mind drifted off, her body a haze of sensation all circling around what this wonderful man was doing to her.

Oh, how she loved him. With every fibre of her being.

And as this realisation filled her, the pulsations that had been building inside filled too, and, with a cry, she felt the pulsations explode, rippling out of her in one long, continuous wave of sensation.

When she opened her eyes, Pepe was gazing up at her, his eyes hooded and glistening.

'That's the most beautiful thing I have ever seen,' he said hoarsely, before rising to kiss her. Pulling her into his arms, he lifted her off the sofa and carried her over to his sprawling bed.

His lips fused to hers, his hands gripping hers above her head, he entered her immediately. But, despite his impatience to be inside her, there was nothing hurried about their coupling. This was tender beyond her imagination.

With her body already fizzing from her earlier climax, she didn't think she was capable of another orgasm, but Pepe knew her so well, knew exactly when to increase the friction to bring her all the way back to the edge.

Clinging to him, she gloried in his fervent control, her heart singing in tune with her body. Pepe might not love her—might never love her—but in this moment he was making love to her as if she meant more to him than just the mother of his child and his lover for the moment. He was making love to her as if she were the most precious thing in his world.

When her climax finally erupted, he was right there with her, his face buried in her shoulder, groaning words in Italian as he drove himself inside her with a final thrust.

'You are crying?' he asked, long minutes later when he eventually lifted his head from her neck.

She hadn't even noticed tears were streaming down her face.

'Did I hurt you?'

She gave a quick shake of her head. 'Hormones' was the most she could utter.

How could she tell him she was crying because she'd done the one thing she'd sworn she would never do?

Far from living together as a couple sating the desire between them, it had shifted it into something deeper.

She had fallen in love with him, and she knew without a shadow of doubt that when the time came for Pepe to call it a day her heart was going to shatter into tiny pieces.

CHAPTER THIRTEEN

'ARE YOU SURE you're okay?' Pepe asked for the third time since they'd left the house. Cara seemed to have lost much of her colour and was much too quiet for his liking.

'I guess I'm a little apprehensive about this exhibition.'

Reaching for her hand, he pulled it over to rest on his thigh. 'I won't leave you alone for a second when we're there, I promise.'

She smiled wanly. 'I know you won't.'

'How did you cope when you worked at the auction house? You had to deal with new people on a daily basis.'

'That was different. It was work and so I could put my professional head on.'

'Maybe you should try that tonight,' he mused. 'If you see all the rich guests as potential clients for when you go back to work—if you go back to work—you might find it easier to cope.'

'It's worth a try,' she agreed non-committally.

Shifting gear, he drove into a street that was officially the beginning of Montmartre. Knowing how much Cara loved to hear about the arrondissement, he began pointing out places of interest, making a mental note to actually take her to them and not just drive past.

She looked so beautiful this evening. But then, she always looked beautiful. Tonight, she'd left her hair down, the red locks spread out over her shoulders like a fan. She was wearing a simple, high-necked, long-sleeved black dress with a wide red belt hanging loosely around the middle, resting on the base of her swollen belly. In the week he'd been away, her bump had grown. For the first time she actually looked pregnant. In his eyes she'd never looked more beautiful.

'Who's the artist exhibiting tonight?' she asked when he turned into the small car park at the back of the exhibition room.

'Sabine Collard. Have you heard of her?'

She shook her head. 'Sabine Collard,' she repeated. He loved the way she tried to pronounce her Rs the French way. It sounded so adorable coming from her Irish lilt.

The gallery was already packed.

Keeping a firm hold on Cara's hand, he guided her through the throng and towards the star of the evening.

When Sabine, a young, angry-looking young lady, spotted Pepe, she embraced him and planted kisses on his cheek.

'Let's stick to English,' Pepe said when Sabine began jabbering in French. He didn't want Cara unable to join in with the conversation.

Sabine gave a Gallic shrug. '*D'accord.* It is very good to see you. I have missed you at the studio.'

Had it been very long? With a jolt, he realised he hadn't visited the studio since Cara had moved in.

'Sabine shares a studio with a few other artists,' Pepe explained to Cara, whose grip on his hand had become vice-like. Casually he rubbed his thumb over her wrist in a wordless show of support.

'So modest!' Sabine exclaimed before addressing Cara directly. 'Your lover owns the studio. It is a *huge* building that was once a hotel. And it is not a "few" artists working and living there—we number fifteen! All living and working rent-free because your lover is one of the few patrons of the art who truly is a patron in all senses of the word.'

'It's not completely selfless,' Pepe hastily explained when Cara's eyes widened. 'I allow them to live and work there rent-free in exchange for a cut of any money they make when they sell their pieces.'

'Five per cent,' Sabine snorted. 'Hardly a big cut, especially when the most of us don't sell anything.'

'I can always raise it,' he warned with a grin.

A beatific expression came over her face. 'Oh, look, there is Sebastien LeGarde. I must socialise.'

Cara watched the chic Frenchwoman sashay away in the direction of a rotund man with the shiniest bald spot she'd ever seen.

Even if she'd been born French she would never have that certain élan Sabine carried off so effortlessly.

'No.'

She looked back at Pepe. 'No what?'

'No, I haven't slept with her.'

'I didn't say you had,' she pointed out primly.

'You were thinking it.' He reached out and gently stroked her cheek. 'There is a chance a couple of my exes will be here though.'

'There's always a chance we'll bump into your exes whenever we step out of the front door,' she said, more tartly than she would have liked.

She had no right to feel jealous. Ever since they'd agreed to make a go of some sort of semblance of a relationship, Pepe had treated her with nothing but respect. Whenever they went out he stuck to her side, his unspoken support worth more than all the money in the world.

He really was nothing like her father and she knew

with as deep a certainty as she'd ever known anything that he would never cheat on her.

All the same, she couldn't help the cloying sickness that unfurled inside her whenever she met his ex-lovers or even made the mistake of thinking about them.

There was a reason jealousy was oft referred to as the green-eyed monster. Thinking of Pepe with anyone else made her go green inside and made the monster within her want to scratch eyes out.

One day soon she would have to find a way to live with it.

She had no idea how she would be able to.

Pepe wanted them to part as friends?

She didn't think she'd even be able to cope with fleeting glances at him. How could *anyone* be strong enough to endure that, to love someone with all their heart and know the recipient would never feel the same way?

All she could do was hold on and hope for a miracle.

Miracles happened. Didn't they?

But even if they didn't, one thing she did know was that she would not behave as her mother had with her father. Whatever happened, Cara was confident her child would never witness the selfish behaviour that Cara had witnessed from *her* parents. Both she and Pepe were committed to that.

Any devastation would take place internally.

'I didn't know you owned a studio,' she said, quickly changing the subject away from something that could easily make her vomit. As she spoke, a sharp stab of pain ran down the side of her belly.

'Are you okay?' Pepe asked, noticing her reflexive wince.

Sucking in a quick blast of air, she nodded.

'You're sure?'

'Yes.' As she reassured him that all was well, it suddenly occurred to her that her back had ached all day. She'd been so excited about Pepe coming home after a week away that she hadn't thought much about it.

'I bought an old hotel a few years back,' Pepe said. 'I had it turned into a home for artists, a place where they could live and work. As you know from Grace, artists often work strange hours. The majority live in poverty.'

'What made you want to do it?' she asked, glad of the conversation to take her mind off irrational thoughts. Besides, she loved hearing anything that helped unlock the mystery that was Pepe Mastrangelo.

His mouth tightened a fraction before he answered. 'There is something incredibly *free* within the art world which I have always felt an affinity with. Growing up in Sicily…it was like living within a straightjacket. It's probably the reason I enjoy flying so much—it gives me a real sense of freedom. Many artists pursue their craft in defiance of their parents' wishes. I wanted to create a space for them to pursue their dream without having to worry about where the rent money was going to come from. Only artists who have been cut off financially from their families are eligible to live there. The only other stipulation is that the artist must have a genuine talent.'

'That's an amazing thing to do,' she said, genuinely touched.

'Not really,' he dismissed. 'It's an investment for me.'

She raised a brow. 'Five per cent?'

He suddenly grinned. 'Georges Ramirez started off in that studio.'

'Really?'

He nodded. 'He was only there for six months before a gallery owner I introduced him to gave him an exhibition and…the rest is history.'

'And does he pay full market rate on the loft?' she asked slyly.

'Near enough,' he said, grinning.

'You never cease to amaze me,' she said with a shake of her head. 'You're always trotting off from country to country on family business, yet you still invest your time as well as your money in the art community.' She gave him a crafty wink. 'How many of your artists have you dropped your kecks for in the name of art?'

His lips twitched. 'Half a dozen. Can I help it if I'm prime model material?'

She sniggered and reached for his hand, lacing her fingers through his. 'Do your family know what you do for the art world?' Somehow, she thought not. Grace would certainly have mentioned it.

He began scanning the room. 'I don't think they would be that interested. My life has never been that much of an interest to them before.' Suddenly he looked back at her with a grin. 'Saying that, they were always interested whenever I got into trouble.'

'Were you a very naughty boy?' she asked, matching his light tone, although she had caught a definite shadow in his eyes.

A gleam now shone in those same eyes. '*Sì*. I was a *very* naughty boy.' He leaned down to whisper into her ear. 'When we get home I'll show you what a naughty boy I can still be.'

Heat filled her from the tips of her toes to the long strands of hair on her head. 'I look forward to it.'

Suddenly filled with the urge to jump onto him and kiss his face off, which, given they were in full view of dozens of people, wouldn't do at *all*, she brought their conversation back to a less suggestive level. 'How come you joined the family business when your heart is clearly elsewhere?'

He shrugged. 'My father died. Luca had been groomed from birth to take over the business but none of us expected my dad to die so young. Luca held the fort on his own while I completed university but I knew he needed me. It wasn't fair for him to shoulder all the burden and pressure on his own. I'd spent my childhood playing the joker and it was time to grow up. Plus it was a good distraction from losing my father and from what Luisa had done to me.'

Her stomach contorted again, although whether this was because he'd mentioned Luisa's name or because of something physical, she didn't know, but it quickly passed.

'I think your father would be very proud if he could see you now, Pepe Mastrangelo.'

His eyes widened a fraction and glistened with something she couldn't discern.

'*I'm* very proud of you. And I know our child will be too.'

Before Pepe could respond, Georges Ramirez joined them, his pretty wife, Belinda, in tow.

Another, sharper pain cut through Cara's stomach.

Blocking out everything around her, she concentrated on breathing through the pain. This was definitely physical.

Cold fear gripped her.

'Not drinking?' Georges asked, looking pointedly at the orange juice in Pepe's hand.

'I'm driving.' Pepe could have used his driver tonight but he enjoyed driving Cara around, especially now she seemed over the worst of her travel sickness. He always made sure to drive her in the car with the sturdiest stabi-

lisers and keep his speed at a steady level—too much
heavy braking and up she would chuck. As good as his
driver was, Pepe preferred to trust in his own driving
ability to keep Cara free from nausea. In any case, it
hardly seemed fair for him to be quaffing champagne
when she had to stick to soft drinks. If she could make
the minor sacrifice of forsaking alcohol for nine months,
then he could do his bit too.

'Good—you can drive me and Belinda home. Stay
for drinks...'

But Pepe had tuned Georges out.

Cara was *proud* of him?

Such a simple word but one that filled his chest with
something so light and wonderful he couldn't begin to
find the words to describe it.

Like a thunderbolt came the realisation that Cara had
the capacity to bring him more joy than anyone else in
the world.

Holding tight to her hand, he scanned the room, looking at some of the women who had once shared his bed
and the women who, if Cara hadn't come into his life,
he would have considered bedding.

There was no comparison, and it was nothing to do
with the physical, although that certainly played its part.

Bedding all these women...

He'd been hiding. Tied up with his feelings of being
second best to his brother and after everything Luisa had
put him through, he'd sworn *never again*. Never again
would he put himself in a position where he could be
hurt. Those women had been nothing but a temporary
affirmation that he was worth something, a good time,
a boost to his ego.

Cara made him feel like a king, as if everything he
did was worth something, if only to her.

At some point he'd stopped hiding the essence of himself from her—he didn't know where or when, it had been a gradual process born of their enforced intimacy over the past few months—and, even after seeing the real man behind the mask, she could still stand there and declare her pride in him.

And it came from her. The one woman in the world whose opinion actually mattered.

Because *she* mattered.

She mattered more than he had ever dreamt possible.

'Pepe?'

Even though he'd successfully tuned Georges out, Cara's whispered call of his name brought him back to sharp focus…and with it came the realisation that something was wrong.

Her hand, still clasped in his with a grip tight enough to cut off his circulation, had gone clammy. In the blink of an eye she had gone from being pale to totally devoid of colour.

He placed a hand to her forehead. It was cold. And damp.

'Cara?'

He'd hardly got her name out when she doubled over with an anguished cry and fell to the floor.

Rancid fear clung to Pepe like a cloak. For the first time in his life he felt helpless. Totally helpless.

The ambulance sped through the streets of Montmartre and he had to stop himself from demanding the driver go faster. The sirens blared but it rang like a dim distant noise, drowned out by the drumming in his head.

Cara's huge eyes, so full of pain and terror, didn't leave his. An oxygen mask had been strapped to her face. He wished he could take her hand but the paramedic had ordered him to keep his distance so she could do her work.

Dio.

Under his breath he said a prayer. A long prayer. He prayed for their child. But mostly he prayed for Cara. For the sweetest, most beautiful woman on the planet, who had brought such meaning and happiness to his life.

Caro Dio, please let him have the chance to tell her how much she meant to him.

When she'd collapsed he'd known immediately something bad was happening. And she had known it too. While they'd waited for the ambulance to arrive, she'd clung to him. He hadn't realised he'd been clinging to her too until the paramedic had prised him off her.

And now it was all out of his hands. Cara's fate and their baby's fate were in the hands of someone else. If anything should happen to her...

Caro Dio, but it didn't bear thinking about.

Cara didn't want to open her eyes. Didn't want to face the reality that opening them would bring.

Soft voices surrounded her then a door shut.

Silence.

She knew exactly where she was. In a hospital. The smell was too distinctive to be anywhere else.

She also knew why she was there.

'Cara?' A tender finger wiped away the single tear that had leaked out.

This time she did open her eyes and found Grace sitting beside her, her face drawn.

'Where's Pepe?'

'He's talking to the doctor. He'll be back soon.'

'I want Pepe.' It came out as a whimper.

Grace clasped Cara's hands. 'He won't be long, I promise.'

'I want Pepe.' This time it came out as an anguished howl.

Although it went against all regulations, Grace climbed onto the bed and wrapped her arms tightly around her, letting Cara sob as if there were no tears left to cry.

Pepe staggered along the corridor, the coffee his brother had given him hours ago still clutched in his hand, cold.

When he got to Cara's room, Grace and Luca came out before he could go in.

'Is she awake?'

'She was. She's sleeping again. Probably the best thing for her.'

He nodded mutely, Grace's words sounding distant and tinny to his ears.

Dimly he was aware of them exchanging glances.

Grace took his hand and clasped it in hers.

When he looked he could see she'd been crying.

'Luca and I have been talking and we think Cara should come home with us.'

'No.' He snatched his hand away.

They exchanged another significant glance.

Luca put his hand on his brother's shoulder and drew him away. 'Pepe, I know you're hurting but Cara needs to be with someone who loves her and that person is Grace. You told me yourself you were only together because of the baby.'

Pepe couldn't even find the strength to punch him.

You were only together because of the baby...

Was that really true? Had that *ever* been true?

He didn't know. His brain hurt too much to think. Everything hurt.

It had all been so sudden.

One minute, everything had been fine. The next…

'Listen to me,' Luca said in a gentle tone he'd never heard him use before. 'It is at times like this a woman needs to be surrounded with love and compassion. Your relationship was only ever temporary. Cara and Grace are closer than sisters. Grace will take care of her. I guarantee it.'

'She's got to stay in hospital for a few more days,' Pepe said dully. 'She's had major surgery. She shouldn't travel.' The obstetricians had delivered their baby via a caesarean section. Cara had been knocked out for it.

He wished he had been knocked out for it too.

'We need to arrange the funeral. She won't want to travel anywhere until we've said goodbye.'

Luca winced at the mention of a funeral.

'What?' Pepe snarled, suddenly springing to life. 'You think I'm not going to give my baby girl a proper goodbye because she was *stillborn*? You think Cara will not want to say goodbye to Charlotte? You think we'll want to forget she ever existed, is that it?'

'No…'

Whatever Luca, who had gone white, was going to say was pushed aside when Grace stepped between them.

'Pepe, please, forgive us. All we want is what's best for Cara, and for you. Nothing more. And you're right— she won't want to go anywhere until after the funeral. When she's ready, she can come to Rome with me. Luca will go back to Sicily to be with Lily.'

'It's what's best for Cara,' Luca added quietly.

Pepe knew his brother was right. Although it ripped his insides to shreds, he knew it.

Cara would want to be with Grace. She wouldn't want to be with him.

He finally jerked a nod. 'Okay,' he said heavily. 'But only if that's what Cara wants. If she wants to stay with me then neither of you are to say anything to change her mind.'

Without waiting for a reply, he strolled into the private room and took the seat by Cara.

She was pale enough to merge into the white sheets.

He was glad she was asleep. At least if she slept she wouldn't have to remember, or, worse, feel.

He would gladly give up every organ in his body if it would take away her pain.

The next time Cara awoke, Pepe was sitting on the private room's windowsill, looking out.

'Hi,' she whispered.

His head snapped round and in a trice he was by her side.

He looked dreadful. Still in the same tuxedo he'd worn to the gallery; what had been an impeccably pressed suit was now rumpled. *He* looked rumpled.

He didn't say anything, just took her hands in his and pressed a kiss to them.

'I'm so sorry,' she croaked.

His brow furrowed, but he didn't speak.

'I keep thinking I should have known something was wrong...'

He placed a gentle finger to her lips and shook his head, his face contorted. 'No,' he croaked vehemently. 'Not your fault. It was a severe placental abruption. Nothing could have been done to prevent it. Nothing.'

She swallowed and turned her head away. Everything inside her felt dry, and so, so heavy, as if a weight were crushing her.

Time passed. It could have been minutes. It could have been hours. She had lost all sense of it.

'Has Grace spoken to you about going back to Rome with her?' Pepe asked quietly.

She looked back at him and mouthed a silent 'no'.

His lips compressed together. 'Grace wants to take care of you. She thinks you will want to be with her.'

More time passed as she looked into his bloodshot eyes. He really did look wretched, and no wonder. Pepe had lost his child too. He was suffering too.

'What about you?' she finally said, dragging the words out. 'What do you think?'

He shrugged, an almost desperate gesture. 'This isn't about me. It's about what's best for you.'

Oh.

Somewhere in the fog that was her brain was the re-membrance that their relationship had only ever been temporary.

Nothing lasted for ever, she thought dully. Nothing.

She had no doubt Pepe would allow her to return home with him if she asked. He'd take care of her as best he could.

But he wasn't asking her to go home with him, was he? He was giving her—them—a way out.

And she knew why.

Every time he looked at her he would be reminded of the loss of yet another child.

And every time she looked at him her loss would double.

He'd loved their baby, not her.

She'd loved them both.

'I need to sleep,' she whispered, disentangling her hand and carefully turning onto her side, not quite turn-ing her back to him.

She could hear his breaths. They sounded heavy. Raspy.

'So you're going to go with Grace?'

She nodded, utterly unable to speak.

It was only when she heard the door shut that the dryness inside her welled to a peak and the tears fell, saturating the pillow.

Incoherent with grief, she was unaware of the needle that was inserted into her arm to sedate her.

CHAPTER FOURTEEN

'ARE YOU SURE you want to do this?' Grace asked as the driver pulled up outside Pepe's Parisian home.

Cara nodded absently, gazing at the place she had called home. The place where she had spent the happiest months of her life. The place where the man she loved was holed up, alone.

'You don't have to do this.'

Cara attempted a smile. 'I know that. I *want* to.' How puny a word *want* sounded when describing the desperate yearning that lived inside her to be with him.

But Grace was right. She didn't have to do this. She could get on the jet that was waiting for them and fly off to Rome. The world would still turn. In time she would heal.

But her heart wouldn't. Without Pepe she doubted she would ever feel whole again.

'Are you sure you don't want me to come in with you?'

Cara shook her head. 'No. I need to do this alone. I want to say goodbye to him properly.' At the graveside Pepe had looked desolate. She'd had Grace on her arm, holding her up. He'd stood apart from them all, shunning even his brother.

She needed to satisfy herself that he was holding up. Who was taking care of *him*? she wondered. His mother was in Sicily taking care of Lily. His brother was already en route back to Sicily, having returned for the funeral. Pepe had rejected his attempts to stay with him, assuring both Luca and Grace that he was perfectly all right, and throwing himself into his work.

But he wasn't all right. He couldn't be. The few conversations they'd had to discuss the funeral arrangements had been almost too painful to recall. He'd sounded empty.

His friends, as lovely as she'd come to accept most of them were, were too wrapped up in their own lives to see beyond the tragedy of what had happened between them on anything but a superficial level. And now that the funeral was over, she suspected those that had been there for him thus far—if he'd even let them be there for him, which she doubted—would fall by the wayside.

She'd held off for a full twenty-four hours before caving in to her need to see him. Her mind was tormented with worries for his state of mind. She'd phoned the house and been assured by Monique that he was working from home. She'd called at the right time—Monique had been put on leave with full pay until further notice. She was only at the house at that time with the ostensible excuse of having to drop some dry-cleaning off. She too was worried for him.

'Make sure you take things easy,' Grace warned kindly.

Two weeks had passed since Cara's baby had been so cruelly taken from her. It would be another four weeks before she'd be allowed to lift anything heavier than a cup of tea. 'I promise. I'll call you when I'm done.'

'No rush. I'll wait at the house.' Since her discharge, Cara and Grace had been staying at the home of a friend of Pepe's who was away on business. 'The jet's ready to leave when we are.'

Swallowing her apprehension, Cara used her key to unlock the front door. The alarms were disabled, so she knew he had to be around somewhere, but only silence greeted her. Heavy, oppressive silence.

Slowly she walked through the ground floor. Everything was just as it had been when she'd last walked through this house, when the future had seemed full of hope, when they'd found a new level of intimacy and she'd believed that maybe miracles could occur.

But there were no miracles to be had.

Nothing had changed but the house felt like a shell of itself.

How could Pepe bear to live here all alone with only his own thoughts for company?

At least she had Grace. She would always have Grace and would for ever be grateful to her best friend for everything she had done for her and continued to do. But all Cara wanted was Pepe. It was his arms she wanted around her, holding her. Just holding her. Sharing their grief.

'Pepe?'

No answer.

'Pepe? It's me. Cara,' she added as an afterthought.

Where was he? Oh, please let him be okay.

There was another reason for her being here.

Taking a deep breath, she entered the garage.

All the stuff was there, exactly where she had left it, still in the boxes. The cot. The dresser. The pram. Even the baby bath. Everything.

The weighty nausea that had lined her stomach for the past two weeks began its familiar roll. She closed her eyes and leaned against the wall for support.

Her baby would never sleep in that cot or ride in that pram.

Her chest heaved as she fought back another fresh wave of tears. So many tears. So much grief. And the man she wanted so desperately to cling to could hardly bring himself to look at her.

Heavy steps came into the garage accompanied by even heavier breathing.

'Sorry, I was on a teleconference,' Pepe said tonelessly.

She opened her mouth to say not to worry. Instead, bile and hysteria rose in her throat. The boxes ripped at her.

'Are you healing well?'

She wanted to say yes, but all she could see were the boxes. 'I don't know what to do with this lot. I just don't know what to do.'

At first he didn't answer. 'I'll keep them here until you decide.'

She jerked a nod, and finally made herself look at him. 'Thank you.'

He raised a shoulder. 'No problem.'

Despite his casual air, she wasn't fooled. Not for a second. Pepe was hurting every bit as much as she.

He looked wretched too, even more so than she'd seen at the graveside, when she'd been too heartbroken and scared to do more than cast him fleeting glances. Scared she would take his hand and offer the support he so clearly didn't want. Scared his grief would make him reject her.

He couldn't have shaved at all since it had happened. The man who took such pride in his trim goatee now had a fully fledged black beard. His eyes were bloodshot and wild. Even his clothes were all wrong. He hadn't dressed. He'd thrown clothes on.

His feet were bare.

She longed to reach out but didn't know…

She didn't know anything. She didn't know how to cross the bridge to him.

What did she think she was doing? Pepe didn't want her there.

He didn't want anyone.

She straightened and inhaled deeply, closing her eyes as she said, 'I need to go.'

She took his lack of an answer as agreement.

Her hand on the door, she turned to face him one last time. 'Be kind to yourself, Pepe.'

Tears blinding her, she walked through the living room, fumbling in her bag for her phone to call Grace, who'd likely not even made it back to the house yet.

'Cara?'

Hastily brushing the tears away with the back of her hand and in the process clonking her nose with her phone, she stopped and slowly turned.

Pepe shuffled towards her, his hand outstretched. 'Don't go.'

Her brow furrowed in confusion.

Her legs too weak to carry her any further, her stomach feeling the strain of being upright for too long, she sank onto the chair right behind her.

When he reached her, he knelt down and placed his hand on her neck. 'I can't bear it,' he said hoarsely. 'I think I could cope if it was just the loss of our baby, but losing you too…'

A sound like a wail echoed in the room. It took the beat of a moment for Cara to realise the sound had come from *her*.

Pepe's face contorted and he looked down to her belly then back up to her face, his eyes searching for…something. 'I know what I'm asking is selfish but, please, *cucciola mia*, please don't go. I'll take care of you. I'll help you heal. Please, just give me the chance to show how much you mean to me and prove how much I love you.'

When Pepe saw the confusion and doubt ringing in Cara's eyes, he almost gave up. It was the tiny spark of hope he also saw that gave him the courage to forge on.

To put his heart on the line. Because if he didn't say it now it would be too late.

'When Luisa aborted our baby—and I believe with all my heart that child was mine—it was the loss of that child so soon after the loss of my father that ruined me. Her lies and deceit were supplementary. I never missed *her*. I'd been in love with a dream that didn't exist—in my own family I'd always felt like a spare part. Luca was the brother who mattered; I was just the spare, and, no matter how much my parents loved me, I always knew that. With Luisa, I dreamt of having my own family where *I* mattered.

'Cara, losing *our* baby has broken my heart. Our child was more than a dream. *You* were more than a dream, and you leaving…it's broken *me*. I don't know how to go on. I'm lost without you. I'm…' His voice went. All the desolation he'd been sitting on for the past two weeks burst through and choked him. He didn't even realise he was crying until Cara wrapped her arms around him and pulled his head to her chest.

She kissed his head, over and over, murmuring sweet words and cradling him with such love and compassion that for the first time in a fortnight a trickle of warmth cut through the ice in his chest.

'Oh, my poor love,' she whispered, her own tears falling into his hair. 'I've been so desperate to be with you.

I thought you wouldn't want me here any more. If I'd known how you felt I would never have gone with Grace.'

He raised his head and found his face being rained upon with her tears. 'I thought you *wanted* to be with her.'

She shook her head. 'I wanted to be with you. Just you. I love you, Pepe.'

'You do?'

What looked like a brave smile broke through her tears. 'How could I not fall in love with you? I always thought love between a man and a woman was about sex and power and humiliation. I had no idea it could be about sex and friendship and support. You're everything to me.'

'I'm so sorry for the way I treated you when you first came to me about the pregnancy. And I'm sorry for the way I treated you in Dublin.'

'I understand. You were helping your brother. While I don't agree with your methods, I can see it was something you felt you had to do for his sake. I would have done the same for Grace.'

'I was terrible,' he stated.

'It's done,' she said gently, 'and if it makes you feel better then know I forgive you. I forgave you a long time ago.'

Pepe hadn't realised how badly he'd needed her forgiveness until another trickle of warmth seeped into his bones. It would be a long time before the cold left him, but with Cara at his side he didn't have to freeze alone. And neither did she. Together they could bring the warmth back.

'A part of me always knew getting involved with you would bring me nothing but trouble,' he confessed.

'Really?'

'*Sì*. And I was right. It wasn't just that you were a virgin or that I felt guilt for what I'd done: I couldn't get you out of my head. The pregnancy came almost as a relief—it meant I had a legitimate reason to keep you in my life without having to acknowledge that my feelings for you ran far further than I could ever admit.'

Her bee-stung lip wobbled. He pressed a finger to it and then the tenderest of kisses. 'I used to tease you about being my concubine or my geisha. I can see now how wide off the mark I was—*I* should be *your* concubine because your needs are all that matter to me. The rest of the world can go to hell. *You* are all that matters to me, and whatever it takes to get us through this whole horrific ordeal I will do. I swear.'

'As long as you're by my side, I know I'll get through it,' she said gently. 'And part of that is you letting *me* help *you*. We can support each other.'

'Do you really mean that?'

'More than anything. I used to think wanting to be with a man meant weakness and that to fall in love would make me lose something of myself. But it hasn't. My mum's life is not mine—and you have shown me that. I know I can survive without you, Pepe. I know I can lead a fulfilling life on my own, but I don't want to. I want to be with you. I want to support you just as you've supported me. I love you. Seeing you alone at the graveside tore me in two.'

'Shall we go on our own tomorrow, to say goodbye together?'

Cara nodded through fresh tears then buried her face into his shoulder. Except these tears didn't feel quite as desolate as all the others had. Pepe's love had given her the hope and desire to see the silver lining on the dark cloud.

Together they would heal each other, and then who

knew where their love would take them? All she knew with bone-deep certainty was that wherever they went, they would always be together, united. As one.

As love.

EPILOGUE

'HAVE I TOLD you how beautiful you look today, Signora Mastrangelo?' Pepe whispered into his wife's ear.

She grinned up at him. 'You're looking pretty spiffing yourself. It's nice to see you've made the effort,' she added with a snigger, referring to the charcoal suit he wore with his salmon cravat.

The priest coughed and they forced their attention back to the proceedings before them. When instructed, Pepe carried baby Benjamin to the font, Cara right by his side.

Of course he'd made the effort today, at their youngest child's christening, just as he had for the christening of their twins. From the corner of his eye he saw a pair of miniature grenades launch themselves up the aisle, quickly followed by his elegant mother, who had been designated babysitter for the day.

A loud voice stage-whispered theatrically, 'Gracie and Rocco are being *very* trying today.'

Titters could be heard throughout the congregation. Luca and Grace were standing at the font with them, their heads bowed, their frames shaking at the precociousness of their eldest daughter, who sat in the front row looking self-important for all her five years of age. Their youngest daughter, two-year-old Georgina, was conspicuous by her absence, no doubt rifling through handbags in the hope of finding sweets. Pepe knew a couple of his artist friends had planned to bring sweets laden with sugar and additives in the hope of watching all the toddlers turn into Scud missiles.

Pepe still felt guilt whenever he recalled turning up at Lily's christening dressed more appropriately for a day out sailing than the baptism welcoming his niece into the world. Looking back, he couldn't believe he'd been so selfish. A child's baptism was one of the most wondrous days for all the family. Instead of appreciating that, he'd deliberately dismissed the event, determined to prove to himself that babies and marriage meant nothing when, in reality, family meant everything.

What a shallow life that had been.

Thank God for Cara.

He would never be able to express the pride he felt in her and the pride she gave in him. He would watch her chatting to clients at the gallery they owned in partnership with his brother and Grace, and which Cara ran, and be awed at her knowledge and the daily battle she fought to unlock her shy tongue and speak coherently. She'd even had another go in his helicopter, a trip that had been aborted after five minutes. Some battles just couldn't be won, and severe motion sickness brought on by helicopter travel was one of them.

Once the ceremony was over, all the guests trickled out and headed to the party being held at their Parisian home.

Pepe, Cara and their children lingered a little longer.

They walked to the altar at the side of the church, which held the memorial candles, Pepe holding a sleeping Benjamin in his arms. Cara gave the three-year-old twins, Gracie and Rocco, some change to put in the donation box, then helped both children light a candle.

'Is this for Charlotte, Mama?' Gracie asked.

Cara's eyes were bright with unshed tears but she nodded and smiled for their daughter.

Then it was their turn. Standing close together, they lit their candles and each whispered private words of love to the child who would for ever live in their hearts.

Once the five candles were lit—Pepe lit one for Benjamin too—he turned to his wife and kissed her, a chaste brush of the lips that sweetened the melancholy of the moment.

Only then did they leave the church, somehow managing to keep a hold of each other as well as their hyperactive toddlers and newborn baby.

In his heart he knew they would always keep hold of each other.

* * * * *

COMING NEXT MONTH FROM

HARLEQUIN *Presents*®

Available April 15, 2014

#3233 SHEIKH'S SCANDAL
The Chatsfield
by Lucy Monroe
The world's media is buzzing as brooding Sheikh Sayed and his harem take up residence at the exclusive Chatsfield Hotel...but an even bigger scandal threatens to break when a stolen night with chambermaid Liyah Amari results in an unexpected complication....

#3234 THE ONLY WOMAN TO DEFY HIM
by Carol Marinelli
Personal assistant Alina Ritchi finds her defiance ignited under the powerful gaze of legendary playboy Demyan Zukov. But when every shared touch sizzles, how long can Alina keep saying 'no' when her body wants to scream 'yes'?

#3235 GAMBLING WITH THE CROWN
Heirs to the Throne of Kyr
by Lynn Raye Harris
When Sheikh Kadir al Hassan promotes long-suffering assistant Emily Bryant to royal bride, he's convinced she'll be deemed so unsuitable he'll successfully avoid the crown. But one kiss forces Kadir to make the ultimate choice: his desert duty, or Emily!

#3236 ONE NIGHT TO RISK IT ALL
by Maisey Yates
Dutiful Rachel Holt has never put a foot wrong...until she reaches for one electrifying night with notorious Greek tycoon Alexios Christofides. But *this* one night has great consequences for them both, especially when Rachel realizes Alex's true identity!

HPCNM0414RA

#3237 SECRETS OF A RUTHLESS TYCOON
by Cathy Williams
There's one thing Leo Spencer's luxurious lifestyle can't give him—the truth about his past. His search for answers leads him to Brianna Sullivan, hidden in the Irish countryside, where she soon proves to be a distraction he never anticipated....

#3238 THE FORBIDDEN TOUCH OF SANGUARDO
by Julia James
Self-made millionaire Rafael Sanguardo *always* gets what he wants...and he wants Celeste Philips. Celeste knows she shouldn't fall for Rafael's practiced charm, yet the more her head tells her to walk away...the more she craves his forbidden touch!

#3239 A CLASH WITH CANNAVARO
by Elizabeth Power
Italian billionaire Emiliano Cannavaro is determined to regain custody of his orphaned nephew from Lauren Westwood—a woman he believes is after only one thing. But innocent Lauren won't give up without a fight—and it promises to be explosive!

#3240 THE TRUTH ABOUT DE CAMPO
by Jennifer Hayward
Matteo de Campo wants to secure a multi-million dollar deal with Quinn's family's company—which means she mustn't fall for his enticing appeal! But when Quinn glimpses his inner demons, she's determined to discover just *who* the real Matteo is....

YOU CAN FIND MORE INFORMATION ON UPCOMING HARLEQUIN® TITLES, FREE EXCERPTS AND MORE AT WWW.HARLEQUIN.COM.

HPCNM0414RB

REQUEST YOUR FREE BOOKS!

2 FREE NOVELS PLUS
2 FREE GIFTS!

PASSION SEDUCTION GUARANTEED

YES! Please send me 2 FREE Harlequin Presents® novels and my 2 FREE gifts (gifts are worth about $10). After receiving them, if I don't wish to receive any more books, I can return the shipping statement marked "cancel." If I don't cancel, I will receive 6 brand-new novels every month and be billed just $4.30 per book in the U.S. or $4.99 per book in Canada. That's a saving of at least 14% off the cover price! It's quite a bargain! Shipping and handling is just 50¢ per book in the U.S. and 75¢ per book in Canada.* I understand that accepting the 2 free books and gifts places me under no obligation to buy anything. I can always return a shipment and cancel at any time. Even if I never buy another book, the two free books and gifts are mine to keep forever.

106/306 HDN FVRK

Name   (PLEASE PRINT)

Address   Apt. #

City   State/Prov.   Zip/Postal Code

Signature (if under 18, a parent or guardian must sign)

Mail to the Harlequin® Reader Service:
IN U.S.A.: P.O. Box 1867, Buffalo, NY 14240-1867
IN CANADA: P.O. Box 609, Fort Erie, Ontario L2A 5X3

**Are you a current subscriber to Harlequin Presents books
and want to receive the larger-print edition?
Call 1-800-873-8635 or visit www.ReaderService.com.**

* Terms and prices subject to change without notice. Prices do not include applicable taxes. Sales tax applicable in N.Y. Canadian residents will be charged applicable taxes. Offer not valid in Quebec. This offer is limited to one order per household. Not valid for current subscribers to Harlequin Presents books. All orders subject to credit approval. Credit or debit balances in a customer's account(s) may be offset by any other outstanding balance owed by or to the customer. Please allow 4 to 6 weeks for delivery. Offer available while quantities last.

Your Privacy—The Harlequin® Reader Service is committed to protecting your privacy. Our Privacy Policy is available online at www.ReaderService.com or upon request from the Harlequin Reader Service.

We make a portion of our mailing list available to reputable third parties that offer products we believe may interest you. If you prefer that we not exchange your name with third parties, or if you wish to clarify or modify your communication preferences, please visit us at www.ReaderService.com/consumerschoice or write to us at Harlequin Reader Service Preference Service, P.O. Box 9062, Buffalo, NY 14269. Include your complete name and address.

HP13

*Harlequin Presents welcomes you to the world of
The Chatsfield—synonymous with style, spectacle...
and scandal! Read on for an exclusive extract from
Lucy Monroe's stunning story SHEIKH'S SCANDAL.
The first in an exciting new eight-book series:*
THE CHATSFIELD.

* * *

THE guest elevators at The Chatsfield hotel in London were spacious by any definition, but the confined area *felt* small to Aaliyah Amari.

"You're not very Western in your outlook," she said, trying to ignore the unfamiliar desires and emotions roiling through her.

"I am the heart of Zeena Sahra—should my people and their ways not be the center of mine?"

She didn't like how much his answer touched her. To cover her reaction she waved her hand between the two of them and said, "This isn't the way of Zeena Sahra."

"You are so sure?" he asked.

"Yes."

He laughed, the honest sound of genuine amusement more compelling than even the uninterrupted regard of the extremely handsome man. "You are not like other women."

"You're the emir."

"You are saying other women are awed by me."

She gave him a wry look and said drily, "You're not conceited at all, are you?"

"Is it conceit to recognize the truth?"

She shook her head. Even arrogant, she found this man irresistible, and she had the terrible suspicion he knew it, too.

Unsure how she'd got there, she felt the wall of the elevator at her back. Sayed's body was so close his outer robes brushed her. Her breath came out on a shocked gasp.

He brushed her lower lip with his fingertip. "Your mouth is luscious."

"This is a bad idea."

"Is it?" he asked, his head dipping toward hers.

"Yes. I'm not part of the amenities."

"I know." His tone rang with sincerity.

"I don't do elevator romps," she clarified, just in case he didn't get it.

Something flared in his dark gaze and Sayed stepped back, shaking his head. "I apologize, Miss Amari. I do not know what came over me."

"I'm sure you're used to women falling all over you," she offered by way of an explanation.

He frowned. "Is that meant to be a sop to my ego or a slam against it?"

"Neither?"

He shook his head again, as if trying to clear it.

She wondered if it worked. She would be grateful for a technique that brought back her own usual way of thinking, unobscured by this unwelcome and unfamiliar desire.

* * *

Step into the gilded world of THE CHATSFIELD!
Where secrets and scandal lurk behind every door…

Reserve your room in May 2014!